Trouble in the Casino...

I spun suddenly and smashed Ernie in the nose with the flat of my palm. I'm not the best brawler in the family—my sister, for one, could kick my ass—but Shana O'Gale's little brother can take care of himself as well.

Ernie reeled back, clutching his face, blood leaking from between his fingers.

Bert turned slowly, surprised by my sudden move. I slammed my foot into his gut, putting as much power into the kick as I could.

Bert flew through the air and crashed against the wall. His big frame made the wall shudder and knocked a small hole in the plaster. The Crock O' Gold casino and I were not getting off on the best terms, but I didn't care.

...To get out of this, you'd need the
Luck o' the Irish

Luck o' the Irish

Stephen D. Sullivan

*

Walkabout Publishing • 2008

Walkabout Publishing
S.D.Studios
P.O.Box 151
Kansasville, WI 53139
www.walkaboutpublishing.com

Cover art & design © 2010 Stephen D. Sullivan

Thanks to Edward, Jean, & Kiff.
And to Paul McComas for the 2010 proof.

ISBN: 978-0-9802086-6-5

For
Augustus H. Sullivan
&
Pearl C. Sullivan—
Long gone, still missed.
and
For the Boston Celtics—
Always.

Contents

ONE
A Chance Meeting

"Name your price," said the politician, smiling broadly in my direction.

I stuffed another forkful of potato skin with sour cream, bacon, and cheddar cheese into my mouth as if I were considering his offer. Congressman Fitzgerald was an influential force in Massachusetts, and Mother O'Gale taught me to give powerful people due respect. In Fitzgerald's case, this respect lasted about ten seconds—which is a lot more than I would have given other pols.

I put the fork down and looked at my watch, my eyes tracing the intricate Celtic knots on its case as I flipped it open. The time read seven past seven in the evening—a good omen. Maybe.

"Sorry," I said slowly, "but it's not for sale."

Fitzgerald smiled as if he couldn't believe he'd heard me correctly. Lines like canyons creased his wide red brow; his bushy white eyebrows knitted together. He pursed his thin lips, and his dark pupils gleamed in small but intense eyes. Clearly he wasn't used to being turned down.

"Now, look, Shawn—do you mind if I call you Shawn?"

I shrugged, as it clearly didn't matter to him whether I minded or not. Politicians tend to do what they want anyway.

"Shawn," he continued, "I've been looking for a watch like that for a long time. It reminds me of one my grandfather brought from Ireland when he first came to this country. I'd really like to have it, and I'm willing to give you anything you think is fair for it. You look tired, like maybe you could use a vacation—are you taking a plane out?"

"No," I said. "Actually, I've taken a fancy to one of the waitresses who works in this little airport bar and grill. Just my bad luck she isn't working tonight." I took another bite of potato skin.

"Well, I'm taking a plane out, and I don't have much time. So, since you could use a vacation, why don't we make a trade. You give me the watch, and I'll arrange to lend you my cottage on the Cape for a week—staff included. Bring your lady friend if you like. If you need, I could talk to your boss, arrange the time off for you."

I chewed carefully, as if considering the offer. Finally, I said, "I'm self-employed."

"A busy man, then?" he asked. I nodded. "Well, okay, then, let's cut the bull. I told you to name your price, and you wouldn't. You don't seem interested in trading either. Surely there's something you're interested in, something a man in my position could give you.

"Do you want to meet the Governor, or the President? I can arrange it. Tax trouble? I can fix it. Just give me a hint here; tell me what it is that you need. What turns you on?"

"Actually," I said, leaning back in my chair, "there is something I rather fancy. . . . I like a bit of a game now and then."

The congressman raised his eyebrows. "Pardon?"

"You know. Games of chance. Gambling."

Fitzgerald's dark eyes lit up, and he smiled a winning, professional smile—one guaranteed to melt the hearts of constituents.

"Well, then," he said. "Name your game." He checked his wristwatch. "It has to be brief, though. I've got a plane to catch."

"All right, then," I said, leaning forward now as if engaging in some great conspiracy. I dropped my voice so only he could hear. "I'll put my watch up against your plane ticket. We'll draw one card from a deck. High card wins. You draw first."

"But you don't even know where I'm going."

I smiled. "I like to go where the wind blows me."

"But I paid full price for this ticket."

"A minute ago, you were willing to pay any price for this watch," I said, dangling the timepiece in front of him on its long chain. The watch sparkled magically in the bar's dim light. I knew I had him.

"All right," he said, gruffly nodding his head. "I suppose you have cards on you?"

"I do, but you can pick up a new deck from the shop next door, if you like."

Fitzgerald nodded. "I'd prefer that."

"Go fetch them, then," I said, leaning back and propping my feet on the barstool between us. "Hurry back."

The congressman frowned and grumbled a bit, obviously not used to running his own errands—especially when a scruffy-looking rogue like me might have done it for him. He puffed to the knickknack shop next to the bar and returned several minutes later with a pack of fresh Bicycles. As he broke the seal, I wiped the last bit of sour cream from my lips and took my feet down.

"Shuffle," I said, trying hard to make it not sound like a command.

Fitzgerald did as he was told, expertly manipulating the deck for a minute or so. He handed the cards to me. I split the pack roughly in half, put the bottom set on the top, and handed the deck back to him.

As he straightened the deck, I said, "You draw first, Congressman."

He put the deck on the bar and carefully selected a card from about a third of the way in. He looked at it and smiled. "King of clubs," he said with smug satisfaction as he showed me the card.

I nodded at him. "My turn, then." I let my hand hover over the deck for a moment or two to build suspense. Then I reached in and plucked out a card from near the bottom of the pile.

As I pulled it out, I turned the card toward Fitzgerald, and the expression on his face told me all I needed to know. I broke into a broad smile as I glanced at the card. "Ace of hearts," I said, trying not to sound too self-satisfied.

11

"Not a magician, are you?" Fitzgerald grumbled as he reached into his coat pocket.

"Nope. Just a lucky guy," I replied, taking the plane ticket from him. I dropped it into the front pocket of my leather Boston Celtics starter jacket while simultaneously stuffing my pocket watch back into my pants. My fist came back out of the pocket with enough money to pay my tab. I dropped the cash on the bar.

Fitzgerald raised his glass to me. "Well," he said, "enjoy your trip."

"I will."

As I left the bar for the parcel locker, he called after me, "Where'd you get that watch, anyway? Maybe I can get another."

"Ireland," I said. "But I'm afraid it's one of a kind."

"Ireland, eh?" he said, his voice fading into the din of the airport as I walked away. "Must be the luck o' the Irish."

When I reached the airport lockers, I fished the key out of my pants and retrieved my Celtics backpack from where I'd left it earlier. As I slung the pack over my shoulder, I pulled out the congressman's ticket and looked at it for the first time.

The words printed on the outside of the boarding pass brought a smile to my lips. Luck of the Irish, indeed. Though I had no idea what fortune had in store for me, at least I now had a destination.

Las Vegas, Nevada.

TWO
Viva, Las Vegas

I closed my eyes, settled my head into the cushion, and listened to the gentle whine of the airplane's engines. It reminded me of the reedy drone of Irish bagpipes. It had been a long time since I'd heard the pipes.

"Honestly," said the woman seated beside me in first class, "I don't know why they can't do something about this infernal noise. It's almost enough to put me off flying. Every time I get into a plane, I say to Mr. Avila, my husband, never again. But of course, here I am—even if he's not."

"Did he have to work, then?" I asked, trying not to sound too interested. I kept my eyes closed.

"Hell, no. Why should he stay home now, when he didn't while we were married? I'm sure he's out catting around somewhere. I, on the other hand, am bound and determined to spend as much of his ill-gotten gains as I can. I'm sure I can make myself happier than he ever did."

"So, where are you headed?" I asked, slitting my eyes open just a bit.

"Where does it look like, honey?" she asked. "Viva, Las Vegas!"

I'd pretty much guessed that from the gaudy blue dress, the permed hair, and the overabundance of jewelry she wore—but it never hurt to ask. At least, it didn't hurt much.

"Well, good luck," I said, leaning back and closing my eyes once more.

Mrs. Avila didn't take the hint. "How much did you bring to lose, honey?"

I took a deep breath and opened my eyes again. "Pardon?"

"To lose at the casinos," she said, "how much money did you bring?"

"Usually, I don't lose," I said.

13

She nodded knowingly. "Professional gambler, then," she said. "So . . . how much do you start with? What's your grubstake?"

I fished into my pocket and pulled out my money—five bills and six coins. "Looks like about nine dollars and fifty-nine cents."

Mrs. Avila looked at me, completely baffled. "You mean you're going to Vegas with less than ten dollars in your pocket? Honey, you'll never get anywhere with that."

"I like to travel light," I said, thinking of the Boston Celtics backpack I had stowed in the overhead compartment. It contained everything I needed when traveling: a change of clothing, toothbrush and toothpaste, condoms, razor. The only other things I required I had on me: a bit of money, comfortable sneakers, loose-fitting clothes, my Celtics starter jacket, and my favorite gold pocket watch. I pulled out the watch and checked the time.

Mrs. Avila fished in her sequined black purse. "There's light, and then there's foolish," she said. "Let me give you something. Just a few dollars. Believe me, I've got more of my husband's 'mad money' than I need. Besides, I'm only going to lose it at the machines."

"You might win at the machines," I said.

She shook her head knowingly. "You ever been to Vegas before?"

"Plenty of times," I said. I don't think she believed me.

She shoved a fistful of dollars toward my face. "Here," she said. "Take it."

"No, I couldn't," I replied. "Don't worry. I'll be fine. I've done this before."

"With only nine dollars?" she asked.

"Less, sometimes."

She looked at me skeptically. "At least take something. I'll worry about you if you don't."

"Well," I said, smiling my best son-you-never-had smile, "if you insist, I'll take one quarter."

"Only one quarter?"

I nodded. "A lot of the machines at the airport don't take half-dollars."

She shook her head and reached into her purse again, putting the rest of the money back. She brought out a single quarter.

I took it graciously. "Thanks." I planted a kiss on her cheek, trying not to end up with a mouthful of make-up.

She smiled and blushed. A look of concern stole over her face. "You're not a gigolo, are you?" she asked.

I chuckled. "No," I said. "That was just a kiss for luck—the luck o' the Irish."

She blushed again. "Oh . . . thank you," she said, her voice almost fluttering. "I'm so glad you aren't . . . a gigolo, I mean. Good luck to you, too."

I leaned back and closed my eyes once again, hoping this time, the black serenity might stick.

"Are you staying with friends?" she asked.

I nodded, but didn't open my eyes. "That's it," I lied. "I'm staying with friends."

"Oh, good," she said. "I didn't want to worry."

She might have kept talking, but that was the last thing I heard before I dozed off.

Some indeterminate length of time later, someone shook me awake.

"Young man! Young man!" said a voice I quickly recognized as Mrs. Avila's.

"Did we crash?" I asked, not immediately opening my eyes.

"Oh, heavens, no," she said. "We've just landed. I didn't want you to miss your friends—the friends you're staying with. I assume they're meeting you at the airport."

I nodded and lied again. "Yes. Thanks. Good luck at the machines, Mrs. Avila."

"And you, too, young man." She paused. "I'm afraid I didn't catch your name."

I opened my eyes and looked at her. "Farrell Shawn O'Gale," I said, my Kelly greens sparkling, "but my friends call me Shawn."

"Well, good luck to you, too, Shawn. I guess you weren't kidding about the luck o' the Irish."

"I never kid about luck," I replied.

Having done her duty in waking me, Mrs. Avila joined the rest of the passengers in their cattle drive off the plane. I waited until the aisle had cleared out, and then retrieved my backpack from the overhead rack.

"Have a great time in Vegas!" a plucky stewardess said as I left the plane.

"You, too," I said, nodding. She was cute, in a plastic way, all hair and breasts. Definitely not my type. At least, not at the moment.

I walked down the jetway, shaking the stiffness out of my legs.

Vegas.

Our landing gate didn't give a view of the city, but even in the backwaters of the airport you knew exactly where you were.

Friendly slot machines stretched out their hands to take your money as soon as you got past the jetway door. They snagged the casual passerby, robbing him of a few coins before letting him continue on his busy way. They were far more effective than street beggars, and cops never asked the machines to move along and do something productive.

Of course, the machines were doing something productive; they were doing the business of Las Vegas. The city's job was to relieve people of their money and make the victims smile about it. Vegas did its job well.

I sauntered over to the nearest machine, pulled out the quarter Mrs. Avila had given me, and dropped it into the slot. It was an old-style machine, one with real tumblers rather than flashing electronic displays. Of course, it was still computer controlled—all the games in Vegas were—harder to beat the odds that way.

I pulled the handle and watched the tumblers spin.

When they stopped, I smiled and scooped up the payout. Fifty dollars. Enough to keep me tripping down fortune's path awhile longer.

Enough for a decent start at the tables.

THREE
AS THE WHEEL TURNS

Vegas loves people with money. If you're gambling and winning, you don't have to pay for anything. Free food, free lodging, and free drinks all dash your way with reckless abandon. Of course, the drinks come to any sucker—the better to decrease your odds of winning. Women come as well, though usually not for free.

So far, I'd been turning the women down, though I'd been taking the free swag. In a country with thousands of homeless, hungry people, the rich get complimentary food, drink, and shelter. Go figure. Viva, Las Vegas.

I'd gotten pretty rich in the week and a half I'd been in town. That initial fifty dollars turned into a hundred, then two hundred, then four. You can do the math after that. First day in I got comp drinks; second day, it was comp meals; third day, a comp room.

I spent the first day at Lady Luck, followed by a day at the Czar's Treasure II. Then I switched to the Vegas Hilton. I always wanted to live the Star Trek experience. When I got tired of 24th century smiles, I settled on the Silver Sands.

The Silver Sands is an old place on the outskirts of the city. People like Donald Trump keep talking about buying it, knocking it down, and putting up something bigger and more profitable— as if taking money from people and giving nothing but neon in return weren't profitable enough.

The Sands doesn't have the most gaming tables in town, or the most slot machines. Their rooms aren't the biggest, or even the best appointed. However, people working at the Sands are friendly, despite constantly fearing for their jobs—or maybe because of it.

Friendly service counts for a lot with me. Besides, I've always preferred to be a big fish in a small pond—that is, when I've felt like being any kind of fish at all.

The pond of my free suite wasn't large by Vegas standards. Two rooms, one large bed, two TVs, a fridge, a bathroom, no Jacuzzi. It met my needs nicely. I probably could have gotten a better suite elsewhere, but as I said, the Silver Sands suited me. I liked the thought that maybe my patronage kept the place from being knocked down for another day or two.

Certainly, people who wanted to reach Farrell Shawn O'Gale had no trouble tracking me down there. Not that I really wanted to talk to any of those people. Mostly, they were trying to sell me things: cars, homes, sex—things I wasn't willing to pay for.

Occasionally, an offer to take in a stage show—on the house, naturally—would wend its way through the switchboard to my suite. The casinos offering the shows hoped I'd stop by after ogling the dancers and blow some of my newfound dough at their gaming tables. Though I often obliged by taking in the show, I seldom fell for the second part of the trap. I always try to be careful where I play games.

After wasting my evening at a particularly mediocre show, I found myself sitting at one of the Silver Sands' roulette tables, trying to change my luck. It was late, even by Vegas standards, and most of the gaming addicts had crawled into their martinis for the night. Those who couldn't leave under their own power, the bouncers politely escorted out. In Vegas, you try to be nice to even the biggest assholes; you can never tell who might strike it big tomorrow.

I like to think people treated me nicely for different reasons—though I'm probably just deluding myself.

Anyway, my delusions and I were sitting at a roulette table, betting small change and watching the place empty out. Usually, I would have gone upstairs much earlier, but the show left a particularly bad taste in my mouth, despite the free booze.

The other reason I'd hung around was that I'd taken a shine to the croupier, a nice young dish named Erin Doyle. She was medium tall, about my age, and had wavy brown hair. She wore the usual Sands' croupier outfit, designed to make the person wearing it as unattractive as possible. Despite this, I could see she had a nice figure to go along with her nice smile. She also had deep brown, soulful eyes.

Okay, so I hadn't been laid in a while, but I don't think either that fact or the booze clouded my judgment—much. I ran my hand through my red hair, leaned back on my stool, and let out a long sigh.

"Tired?" Erin asked.

"Getting that way."

"You know, the management wouldn't want me to say this—some of our best suckers are tired and drunk—but you should get some rest."

I nodded. "I know I should. Probably I should blow town altogether. I think Vegas is starting to wear on me."

"Wear on you?" she said, looking surprised. "But, you've been winning every night since you came here. I've never seen you leave with less money than you came with."

"Even winning can get tiring," I said. I pulled my gold pocket watch out and flipped open the lid. It was late. I flipped the watch closed and put it back in my pocket.

She smiled at me in disbelief. "You're bullshitting me. Nobody, but nobody, gets tired of winning. Not in Vegas."

I shrugged. "I do. Winning isn't everything. Vegas isn't everything."

She laughed, and then covered her mouth and looked at the local security camera. It wouldn't do for the casino to see their staff having too good a time.

"I don't think I've ever met anyone like you," she said. "Not here, anyway. Maybe in LA ... "

"You from LA?" I asked.

"No," Erin said. "I'm from Missouri. I came west to work."

"Acting?" I said.

She nodded and shrugged. "Same old sad story. I wanted immediate recognition of my talent and a meteoric rise to fame. Money. Mansions. Fast cars. Hunks in thong Speedos. Instead, I got a one-room walk-up and a lot of bad passes from producers who didn't even have real roles to offer. LA . . . Just not enough good times to go with the sleaze."

"As opposed to Vegas?"

"I don't mind a bit of sleaze if the money is right."

"At least you landed on your feet," I said.

"As opposed to my back?" she replied playfully. "Yeah, I guess so. If you can call this place 'feet.' At least it's an honest job."

That made me smile. "Is gambling an honest job?"

"For me it is. How about you?"

"I try never to do anything entirely honest," I said. "Too much like work."

She shook her head to straighten her hair. It fell in pleasing curls down around her shoulders. "Well," she said, leaning forward over the table, "I hate to say this, but if I don't spin this thing, they'll reassign my table. You wanna play any more, or you gonna move on?"

"I might give it one more roll, if the stakes were right."

"How do you mean?" she asked.

"How've you done this evening? Meeting your quota?"

She frowned. "No. It's been slow tonight. Not enough suckers. I'm a bit short, and my shift is nearly over." She looked at the camera again. "They'll be pissed, but I'll be okay. I've had a pretty good week. It averages out in the end. I worked over at Czar's Treasure II for a while. Let me tell you, it was feast or famine over there. All Romanov thinks of is money. Make your quota, and you're a queen. Come up a bit short and . . . I swear, that Russian would sell his own mother if he thought it'd make him a nickel." She sighed. "At least they're more reasonable over here."

21

I nodded. "Well, maybe I should help you make your quota for these reasonable people, and then we could have coffee or something."

"Ha!" she said. She looked around to make sure no one was listening. She leaned toward me and whispered, "You, you cute bastard, are half the reason I'm short tonight."

I shrugged. My kelly-green eyes twinkled. "Hey, what can I say? I'm just a lucky guy."

"Too lucky," Erin said. "It's not natural."

"Nope, it's not," I said, smiling. "Luck o' the Irish."

"So," she said leaning back and assuming her professional demeanor, "you gonna take another spin, or should I tell my boss to cash me out early?"

"You up for coffee?"

"Maybe," she said. "You win, and I'll definitely call it a night."

"I'll take another spin."

I put chips worth five hundred dollars on twelve and black. Erin spun the wheel.

The ball ran down the track and clattered across the numbers: red, black, high, low. The wheel slowed, the numbers became visible: eighteen, seventeen, sixteen. The ball skipped across the wheel: fifteen red, fourteen black, thirteen red. It came to a stop.

Thirteen red.

"You lost!" Erin said, unable to contain her shock.

"Happens to the best of us."

"You never lose. I've never seen you lose."

"Just because you've never seen me lose doesn't mean it doesn't happen. You up for coffee?"

She arched one eyebrow at me. "You gonna play anymore?"

"Not roulette," I said.

She smiled, and her brown eyes twinkled. She said, "I'll cash out."

FOUR
HIGH ROLLERS

Erin got out of my shower and dried her curly brown hair. I admired her naked back. I've always liked a well-sculpted back.

"You know," she said, "I don't usually do things like this. If I usually did things like this, I would have gotten a lot farther than I did in LA."

She glanced back at me over her shoulder. "You believe me, don't you?" she asked.

I leaned back on the bed. "Mother O'Gale taught me never to doubt the word of a lady."

Erin smiled and pulled on her jeans. She'd changed out of her croupier uniform before we went out for coffee. "Well, that's good," she said. "Because I'm really not into one-night stands."

"Neither am I," I said.

"Well, good." She pulled her T-shirt over her head. "Which is not to say I think this is some kind of long-term thing. I've been in Vegas too long to think that."

"Me, too," I agreed.

"It's just . . . what I'm saying is . . . tonight was fun. I had a good time. Maybe we could have some more good times. Not that I'm trying to pressure you into anything."

"I had a good time, too," I said. "I like good times. If I didn't, I wouldn't be in Vegas."

Erin laughed, a short vocal explosion. "Ha! You came to Vegas to make money. I've seen you at the tables; you're good. You're probably up here every couple of months." She tucked the shirt into her jeans and sat on the edge of the bed next to me.

I leaned back and adjusted the pillow under my head. "Honestly, Erin, a couple weeks ago, I had no idea I'd be in Vegas at all."

She looked at me with her deep brown eyes. "Bullshit, Shawn," she said sweetly. I leaned forward and kissed her.

"No, honestly," I said.

"You're a professional gambler," she said. "You've got to be."

"I'm just a lucky guy who happens to like a game now and then."

She kissed me back. "You're a liar, Shawn O'Gale. But I've had a good time. Thanks."

"You're welcome. Care to keep the streak going?"

"How do you mean?"

"I'm tired of Vegas," I said, "at least for the moment. How'd you like to go to Lake Tahoe with me for the weekend?"

"To gamble?" she asked.

"Hell, no," I said. "To relax, enjoy the scenery, spend some of my ill-gotten gains, and fool around."

She smiled, sat upright on the edge of the bed, and looked thoughtful. "Well, I do have this weekend off . . . "

"Did I tell you I was lucky?" I said, my green eyes flashing.

She stood. "Shit. Okay. What the hell. I'll go home and pack."

I reached over to the nightstand and checked my gold pocket watch. "Meet me back here in an hour?" I said.

"Better make it two," she said. "I take forever to pack."

I sat up and smiled at her. "Great. Two hours it is. I'll rent a car."

Her face fell. "You mean you don't have a private jet?" She smiled to show she was joking.

"Maybe by the end of next week," I said. I rose and gave her a good-bye hug and kiss.

We lingered together a moment. Then, she pulled away and headed for the door. She opened the door and went out, waving her fingers at me as she left.

"Hurry back," I said.

The door clicked shut. I showered, shaved, and dressed: Celtics socks, jeans, Boston Garden T-shirt, and my leather

Celtics starter jacket. Then I went downstairs to arrange a rental car. I took my Celtics backpack with me, figuring I might want to take a drive before picking Erin up. The pack is my survival gear and my security blanket. With it, I can go anywhere.

By the elevators, just outside one of the gaming rooms, I ran into Mrs. Avila, the divorcee I'd met on the plane from Boston to Vegas. Her powdered face lit up as she saw me.

"Mr. O'Gale!" she said, dashing across the room to embrace me. She smelled of too much perfume. Her jewelry rattled like a snake when she hugged me. I politely pried her off.

"Honestly, Mr. O'Gale," she said breathlessly, "I don't know how to thank you."

"Thank me for what?" I asked.

"The luck o' the Irish," she said. "You told me it would rub off on me, and it did. I've been hitting the slots ever since I got off the plane. It's a miracle."

I chuckled. "Usually, lapsed Catholics don't perform miracles. The church reserves that for higher powers."

"You're right, of course," she said, blushing slightly. "Anyway, I don't know how you did it, but I can never thank you enough."

"I'm glad you've had a good run," I said.

"Better than good. I've already paid for next year's trip, and the trip after that as well."

I nodded. "Just be sure you don't press your luck, Mrs. Avila."

"Oh!" she said, as if startled by the concept. "Do you think I could? What would you do? You've done me such a good turn so far."

"I try never to press my luck."

She frowned. "Maybe you're right. Maybe I should go to Hawaii next year instead."

"Well, if you do, don't tell Vegas I scared you away."

She laughed. "Mr. O'Gale, you are the wit. Well, I must be running. I've met some people, and we're going to have lunch together at Circus Circus. You could join me if you like."

"No, thank you. I have an appointment of my own."

"Well, I won't keep you, then. I hope your luck has been as good as mine. Enjoy the rest of your stay." She bustled toward the front door.

I waved. "You, too," I said.

She disappeared into a cab, her jewelry still rattling.

I sighed and turned back toward the car rental desk. I found myself looking into someone's chest.

The someone was at least six and a half feet tall and as wide as a football player. I looked up. Atop the body sat a squat, pumpkinlike head, sporting two days' growth of beard. The face frowned at me.

"Excuse me," I said, taking a step sideways.

Another goon stepped out from behind the first, blocking my progress. The second man looked similar to his buddy: same gorilla frame and face, though a bit taller and thinner. Both men wore gray pinstripe suits, carefully cut to fit their gargantuan frames. Their appearance screamed hired muscle.

"Mr. O'Gale?" said the first goon.

I nodded, trying to spot a quick way out of the room.

"Our boss wants to see you," said the second goon.

I took a step back so that I was looking at something other than pectorals. "Who's your boss?" I asked. My search for convenient exits hadn't panned out. The goons had me trapped between the casino and the lobby. There were enough people around to prevent violence, but no easy way to escape.

"Mr. Rodrigo Botticelli," said the first goon, who I'd decided bore some resemblance to Ernie on Sesame Street: he had big ears and a round face, and a short mop of hair on top.

"Never heard of him," I said, turning to go.

Ernie's partner cut me off.

"Mr. Botticelli owns the Crock O' Gold casino," said Bert.

"Still don't know him," I said. I started to wish Mrs. Avila hadn't left so quickly. Ernie and Bert had backed me toward one side of the hallway. I began to think I wouldn't get out of this without making a scene.

"Well, he knows you," said Ernie. "And Mister B wants to see you. Now."

"Look," I said. "I don't know you, I don't know your boss. If he wants to see me, he can call the desk and make an appointment. Right now, I've got some personal business to attend to. So, if you don't mind . . . "

With that, I strode forward, pushing my way between the two hulks. They didn't reach out to stop me. I was pleasantly surprised.

"That weekend in Tahoe ain't gonna happen," Bert called after me.

I turned back toward the two of them.

Ernie smiled—a toothy, loathsome grin—and said, "We got your lady friend."

FIVE
IN THE CARDS

I spun suddenly and smashed Ernie in the nose with the flat of my palm. I'm not the best brawler in the family—my sister, for one, could kick my ass—but Shana O'Gale's little brother can take care of himself as well.

Ernie reeled back, clutching his face, blood leaking from between his fingers.

Bert turned slowly, surprised by my sudden move. I slammed my foot into his gut, putting as much power into the kick as I could.

Bert flew through the air and crashed against the wall. His big frame made the wall shudder and knocked a small hole in the plaster. The Crock O' Gold casino and I were not getting off on the best terms, but I didn't care.

*

I'd put up with some rough treatment as Bert and Ernie—my pet names for the casino's goons—hustled me into a waiting car outside my hotel. I played it cool when they brought me to the Crock's back entrance and to Rodrigo Botticelli's private elevator.

I kept my eyes open for exits, but I went along with the game. I had to. Somewhere, Bert and Ernie had my lady friend, Erin, hostage.

As I walked through one of the Crock's "Employees Only" corridors on my way to Botticelli's office, I found myself getting pissed. I'd been looking forward to that weekend in Tahoe with Erin, even if we had just planned it a couple of hours before. The famous O'Gale "Irish" began to rear its fiery head. I didn't like being pushed around. I liked it even less when people pushed my friends around.

I wondered what the goons had done to Erin. I hoped she was okay, but I decided to make Bert and Ernie pay, either way.

I guess I was so lost in thought that I slowed down as I walked to Botticelli's office. Ernie gave me a shove. "Mister B is waiting for ya," he said.

I decided to see Mr. B on my terms rather than his.

I shoved back, which is how we got to where we were.

*

Ernie dropped his hands from his face and balled them into fists. Blood leaked out of his nose and dripped off his chin, spattering crimson polka-dots onto his tailored gray suit.

He swung at me with a roundhouse right. I ducked and jabbed him in the midsection. It was like hitting granite.

He followed up with a left; I didn't get out of the way quick enough.

The blow barely clipped me on the side of the head, but it was enough to send me staggering backward. My left ear burned where he'd hit me. Ernie smiled and came in again. Bert got up off the floor and followed him.

I began to think that this fight hadn't been such a good idea after all. I blinked back the flashbulbs going off behind my eyes and ducked just in time to avoid another blow from Ernie's ham-sized right fist.

I darted under his arm and found myself face to face with Bert. Bert grabbed for me, but I spun out of the way. I knotted my fingers together and brought my hands down on Bert's back as hard as I could.

He fell right into Ernie; the two of them got tangled together. For a moment all I could see was flailing gorilla arms. That moment was all I needed.

I sprinted to the door at the end of the hall. It had *Botticelli* printed on a gold plaque on the front. I yanked the door open and slipped inside. I found myself in a plainly furnished outer office. A secretary's desk sat on one side of the room; on the other, a leather couch waited for visitors.

The room was empty; the secretary must have been on a coffee break. Glad for my luck, I locked the door I'd just come through. I could hear Bert and Ernie barreling down the hall as I did so.

A carved oak door waited on the far side of the room. I figured it must lead to Botticelli's inner sanctum. I walked across the room and opened the door. I wasn't prepared for what I found inside.

Nothing.

Just a two-way TV monitor, a card table, and a folding chair. An unopened pack of cards rested on the table. On the monitor, I saw a pair of black-gloved hands shuffling a different deck.

"Farrell Shawn O'Gale," said a deep voice from the TV monitor. "I was expecting you. Please sit down."

"I'll stand, if you don't mind," I said.

"Suit yourself," said the voice. It had been altered electronically.

"Mister B, I presume," I said.

"Correct," said the voice. The hands on the monitor stopped shuffling. They flipped over the top card and laid it on a green felt table on the other end of the video link.

"The Fool," Mr. B said, indicating the card he'd turned over. "That would be you—a fitting choice, don't you think?"

"I've never much liked the tarot," I said.

"I know," said Mr. B's disembodied voice. "Easier to cheat at cards than to cheat fate."

The hairs on the back of my neck bristled. "I don't cheat," I said.

"So you say," replied Mr. B. "Let's see what the cards say." He turned over the next card, putting it atop the Fool. "The Lovers," he said. "That would indicate your lady friend."

"Where is she?" I asked, feeling my temper rise again.

"All in good time, Farrell. All in good time."

"Shawn," I said. "Nobody calls me Farrell,"

"I think *I* will," observed Mr. B. He turned over the next card and placed it crosswise over the previous two. "The High Priestess," he said. "Hidden forces holding sway over your life. That would be me."

"Look, let's cut to the chase," I said. "What do you want from me?"

The hands turned over another card. "The King of Cups," said Mr. B. "You've benefited from someone's generosity. That's the source of the problems you have now."

"I'm not here to play games," I snapped. "Either you tell me what's going on right now, or I'm out of here."

"Do you think that's the best strategy?" Mr. B's electronic voice asked calmly. "Is that the best strategy for Erin?"

I didn't leave.

Another card. "Four of Swords, inverted. Patience will be rewarded—though the time for that is growing short."

Reflexively, I pulled out my gold pocket watch and checked the time.

Mr. B drew a card and placed it above the Fool. "The Hanged Man, inverted. Arrogance will lead to your downfall. Be careful, Farrell O'Gale."

Before I could react, the gloved hands turned over another card, laying it to the right of the Fool. "One more, for now, I think," the electronic voice said. "The Wheel of Fortune, inverted. In the future, your fortunes will be reversed. The past is catching up to you, Farrell."

"Okay," I said. "I've gone along with your little game. Now cut the bullshit. You've got Erin, and I want her back. Tell me what you want."

"I'd like you to come visit me at my casino headquarters in Reno," said Mr. B.

"No dice," I replied. "You can tell me what you want right here and now."

"Tell you what," Mr. B said. "We'll cut cards for it. If I win, you come to visit me in person. If you win, I'll give you your lady friend back. We can use the deck on the table in front of you. Open it, Farrell."

This setup stank to high heaven, but I didn't see any way out. I picked up the sealed cards from the table and opened them.

"Look through the deck. Assure yourself that it's normal. Then give it a good shuffle."

I rifled through the deck. Hearts, clubs, diamonds, spades, the usual numbers and quantities. It looked ordinary enough. I gave the deck a shuffle and placed it facedown on the table.

"Cut once for me, please," said Mr. B's voice.

"Who draws first?" I asked.

"You do," he replied.

"Then, I suppose, you draw from a deck on that monitor," I said, thinking I saw the catch.

"No. You can draw for me as well—after you draw for yourself."

I frowned. This wasn't the usual con. I couldn't figure out what Botticelli was driving at. Still, there seemed to be nothing to do but play along.

I cut the deck and then drew a card. I turned it toward the camera mounted atop the monitor before looking at it myself:

Jack of Hearts.

I smiled just a bit.

"Now for me," Mr. B said.

I let my hand hover over the deck, but something didn't feel right.

"Quickly, please, Farrell," said the voice. "Pick a card and flip it over on the table. We haven't got all day."

I reached into the deck, pulled out a card, and flipped it over onto the tabletop.

Queen of Clubs.

Shit.

"Okay," I said. "You win. What next?"

"My associates will take you to the airport where a private plane will convey you to my main office," said Botticelli.

"And Erin? What about her?"

"She won't be harmed, I assure you. I really have no interest in her. It's you I want to see."

I nodded. "Okay, let's get to it."

"See you soon, Farrell." The monitor switched off.

I knew I'd been set up, but I had no idea how.

The only thing to do was to head for Reno with Mr. B's associates.

Listening to Bert and Ernie pounding on the door of Botticelli's outer office, I doubted it would be a pleasant trip.

SIX
UPS AND DOWNS

"Not so smart now, are you?" Ernie asked, his voice growling over the noise of the airplane's engines.

I looked at the valley yawning below my head and hoped Ernie had a good grip on my leg. Surviving a fall from ten thousand feet might be pressing my luck just a bit.

"Quit fooling around and bring him back into the airplane," Bert said from behind the controls. "We ain't bein' paid to kill this O'Gale character."

"The little shit broke my nose," Ernie said.

What could I say? I'd given it my best shot, and the bandage on Ernie's face *did* improve his appearance.

"I'm sure Mr. Botticelli doesn't want me splattered all over the landscape before I can speak to him," I said, trying to sound a lot braver than I felt. My stomach had begun to feel the effects of being dangled upside down out of the open door of the single-engine plane that Bert was piloting.

"Shut up, you!" Ernie barked at me.

"I ain't kiddin'," Bert said. "Bring him back in the plane before something happens that we'll both regret. You've had your little joke. Besides, you don't want Mr. B mad at us, do ya?"

That set off something in Ernie's simian brain. Slowly, he pulled me back into the aircraft.

"Thanks," I said, not meaning it. "I'm sure your employer will appreciate it."

"Shut up, O'Gale!" Ernie said, pushing me into one of the plane's four seats. It was the same one I'd occupied before his little "prank." Ernie took the copilot's seat in front of me, glowering as he sat down.

I looked around. Night blanketed the plane, though the moon shone brightly outside. Below us, the Amargosa Desert yawned, and the aptly named Funeral Mountains stretched into the darkness. It was a long way down, and I shivered slightly to think I'd almost taken the express elevator to the bottom. Whatever else Mrs. O'Gale might have wanted for her son, Shawn, I felt sure that being a pancake was not part of her plans for my future.

I took a deep breath and swallowed hard.

Seeing my discomfort, Ernie smiled his toothy smile.

"Get a load of the hero," he chuckled to Bert.

Bert wasn't listening. He had an evil gleam in his eye. Ernie must have noticed something because he turned just as Bert produced a butterfly knife from within his gray pinstriped suit.

Bert flicked the knife open with his left hand and stabbed it at Ernie's gut. Ernie grabbed Bert's wrist with both hands and stared, shocked, at his partner.

"What're ya doin'?" Ernie asked.

Unwilling to sit quietly for murder, I jumped forward, but Bert clouted me aside with one ham-sized fist. I fell back into my seat, the impact jarring something loose from the overhead rack. It fell into my lap, taking my breath away.

"Sorry about this," Bert said, in a tone that made it clear he wasn't sorry at all. "Somebody made me a better offer."

Ernie reached up and kicked Bert with one big foot. Bert fell back into the plane's control panel. The instruments sparked, and the plane veered to port. Neither combatant seemed to notice.

"Mr. B ain't gonna like this," said Ernie.

"I don't give a shit what Mr. B likes," said Bert. "I ain't working for him no more." He threw the knife. It stuck in Ernie's left shoulder. Ernie gasped in pain. Bert braced himself and kicked Ernie with both feet.

Ernie flew back against the door of the plane. The door popped open. Ernie fell out into the darkness. He didn't even scream.

Bert grabbed the plane's controls, trying to straighten her out.

Recovering my wits, I looked at the parcel that had fallen into my lap: a parachute. Just what I needed. I smiled. After a temporary setback, the O'Gale luck was running true to form again.

Bert glanced back at me. "Oh, no you don't!" he snarled. He hadn't had much luck with the plane's controls, and now he ignored them completely. The controls started to smoke.

The plane danced wildly as Bert lunged over the seat at me. "I ain't gonna lose my meal ticket!" he bellowed. He grabbed for me. Foolishly, I put the parachute between us. Bert seized the parachute and yanked. I forgot to let go.

I flew toward the front seat and banged my nose against the headrest. My nose began to bleed.

"I think," I said, sounding as though I had a terrible head cold, "flying the plane might be more important at the moment."

Bert looked at me as though he agreed. Then he socked me across the jaw. Light bulbs flashed before my eyes, and I slumped against the back of the seat.

Bert went back to struggling with the controls. The plane straightened a bit, but the cockpit was rapidly filling with smoke. Bert began to cough. He glanced back at me and spotted the parachute.

"Screw the money," he said. "Gimme that parachute!"

He grabbed it, but I refused to let go. The smoke had entirely filled the plane now. I could hardly see Bert through the haze. Both of us were coughing like crazy.

I heard Bert swing at me, and above my head the seat shuddered. I hung onto the parachute with my left hand and, with my right, groped for something to clobber him with.

In the smoke-choked darkness, my hand found the shoulder strap of my Boston Celtics backpack. There weren't any weapons inside, just some essential supplies for my wanderings, but the pack was big and heavy, a useful bludgeon. I grabbed it and swung it toward where I figured Bert's head must be. Astoundingly, I connected.

Bert let go of the parachute. He groped in the darkness, found my backpack, and yanked it out of my hands.

"Got it!" he cried.

That seemed like my cue to bail out. I opened the door next to me and rolled into the open air.

Fortunately, I'd done some parachuting before. Sister Shana had taken me on a jump for my twenty-first birthday, God bless her. I pulled on the parachute as the plane sailed away overhead, leaking smoke as it went. I yanked the ripcord and prayed the chute had been packed right.

It had. The chute opened perfectly, billowing into the moonlight like a huge white jellyfish. I looked down.

The desert yawned below me—thousands of acres of perfect landing area. I picked a likely spot and glided to the ground.

As my feet touched down, I saw a fireball where the airplane hit a mountain. I don't know if Bert made it out, but if he did, I bet he didn't have much luck getting my backpack to open into a chute.

Too bad.

I liked that backpack.

SEVEN
COYOTE LUCK

If you ever have to pick a place to parachute into, Death Valley is both a good choice and a bad choice.

It's a good choice because, being a desert, there aren't too many things to run into—nasty, arm-breaking things, like trees and huge boulders.

On the down side, it's a stinking desert, and if you miss one of the roads running through it, you're pretty much on your own. Having the luck o' the Irish, I didn't get hurt when I parachuted out of the burning airplane. I found some nice soft sand dunes to land in.

However, I was completely screwed in terms of landing near a road. I stood on top of my dune and looked around. Mountains and scrub desert to the east and more dunes west.

Now, my sister Shana probably would have known what to do in a situation like this. She'd been all over the world poking her nose into things that were nobody's business. In doing so, she'd gotten into every imaginable kind of fix—and come out of those tight spots wiser and sometimes wealthier. She would have known how to get out of a sticky situation like this. Hell, she had probably even told me what to do in a predicament like this.

Of course, being the dutiful little brother, I wasn't listening.

For a moment, I wished I had less luck and more of my sister's smarts—but only for a moment.

I knew a little bit about the area. I'd even been through Death Valley National Park once on my way to California. I figured that what I was looking at was the Last Chance Mountains—appropriately named, in this case.

I had driven a road somewhere near those mountains. I hoped I could find that road before the sun turned me into a baked potato. Fortunately, there was still plenty of moonlight to help me on my way.

Wary of Shana's "you never know what you'll need" maxim, I packed up the chute and slung it on my back. Then I headed east.

People who have never walked on sand have some inaccurate notions about it. They've seen dozens of sappy romantic commercials and watched some busty Baywatch girl run on the beach. Sand is fun. Sand is sexy.

Sand sucks.

It takes twice as much effort to walk on sand as it does on dirt. That's why Marvelous Marvin Hagler used to go running on the dunes of Cape Cod when he was in training. Great fighter, Hagler.

Me, I'm just lucky. Most of the time. Didn't feel lucky walking over the dunes, though.

Soon I had shinsplints, and my calves were burning like hell. The mountains still seemed a long way off. I checked my pocket watch, admiring the intricate tracery on its gold cover only for a moment before opening it and reading the face. 4:30 a.m.

Shit. Sunrise would be coming soon, and walking in the stinking desert in the sun didn't conform to my idea of fun. I wished I had my backpack—which had some snacks and bottled water inside—but it had gone down with the plane.

I decided to stop a minute. I took the parachute off my back, propped it on a dune, and leaned against it. The moon was setting, and the shadows before me grew longer by the minute. I looked at the mountains and cursed.

I wondered if I could make a tent out of the chute to keep the sun off me. I thought maybe I could.

I wished I had something to eat.

I wished I was back in my hotel room at the Silver Sands.

I wished my new friend, Erin, and I had gone to Lake Tahoe for the weekend.

I wished she hadn't been kidnapped by the mysterious Mr. Botticelli.

I wished I'd never taken that plane ride with Mr. B's goons. I even wished the goons had just taken me to Reno rather than betraying each other and getting into a big fight.

I wished the plane had never crashed—though I was profoundly grateful to have gotten out before it did.

I wished I had a drink.

As I sat there piling up wishes like it might do me some good, I spotted some movement atop the next dune.

I strained my eyes, peering into the shadows, and a lupine form took shape.

A coyote.

I frowned. "What in hell are you doing out here, boy?" I asked.

Now, I didn't expect the coyote to answer, of course. I've seen a lot of strange and wonderful things in my life, but I don't number talking animals among them. Heck, I figured that just the sound of my voice would drive the thing off. It didn't.

Instead, the coyote slunk down the dune toward me. It didn't look threatening, particularly, though it did look hungry—a trait both of us shared. It looked at me with intelligent blue eyes.

Some American Indians thought the coyote a god: the king of tricksters. He was similar to Loki in the Norse myths, though not as much of a shithead. Hermes from the Greek myths isn't quite an apt comparison, either—though maybe closer than Loki.

I guess in some ways Coyote was like the Irish faeries, capricious and unknowable. At times, he would dispense valuable lessons and wisdom; at other times, he was just a pain in the ass. I wondered which incarnation this animal would be for me: son of a bitch or savior?

The coyote sat down about twenty feet from me, cocked his head, and panted.

"You know," I said, "if we don't get out of this stinking desert, one or both of us is going to die."

Maybe it was my imagination, but I would swear that the coyote nodded at me.

I smiled. "Okay," I said, "if we're going to spend some time together, we might as well introduce ourselves. I'm Farrell Shawn O'Gale. My friends call me Shawn."

The coyote pawed the ground and made kind of a yawning/barking sound. Lassie he wasn't.

We eyed each other warily for a minute. Maybe he guessed that I was calculating how long a man in the desert might survive on coyote meat. Probably, he was figuring the same thing about me.

Finally, I broke the silence. "The way I see it," I said, "one of us is likely to end up as a meal for the other before this is all over."

The coyote yawned in agreement, giving me a nice look at his canines.

"Tell you what," I said, reaching into my pocket. "I'll roll you for it." I pulled out a pair of regulation dice and showed them to the animal. "Vegas craps rules," I said. "I throw a winner or make point, I eat you. I crap out, you eat me. Whatta you say?"

The coyote threw back his head and howled. I took that as a "yes."

I smoothed out a spot in the sand between us for the center shooting area. Then I cocked back my arm and rattled the dice in my closed fist.

The coyote watched me in rapt attention.

I brought my arm forward and let fly. The dice sailed through the air and tumbled across the sand.

Before they could stop rolling, the coyote pounced.

At first, I thought he was coming for me. I jumped back, my arms coming up reflexively to protect my face and neck. But the coyote didn't have a Shawn O'Gale supper on his mind. Instead, he scooped up the dice in his mouth and dashed over the top of the nearest dune.

I got to my feet and ran after him, but he had disappeared into the night.

"Stopping the roll is an automatic forfeit!" I called after the animal. "You owe me your life!" He didn't come back. "Welcher!" I yelled. The desert swallowed up the echoes.

I sat down and let out a long breath, unsure whether to miss the company or to be glad had I escaped alive. I felt exhausted. After the day's excitement, I guess I must have dozed off without realizing it.

The sun beating down on my red hair woke me. There was something else as well: a sound. I realized with a start that the sound belonged to an automobile engine.

I sprang to my feat and rushed to the top of the nearest dune. In the distance, I saw a cloud of dust coming my way rapidly.

Leaving my parachute behind, I ran in that direction. Not many dunes over, I came to a road. The sand had nearly obliterated the path, but it was a road, sure enough. I staggered down onto it and looked south.

A Humvee came barreling toward me out of the desert heat.

I raised my hands over my head and waved frantically, trying to get the driver's attention.

As the Humvee came closer, I could see a woman behind the wheel. She had the Hummer's top down, and her long black hair billowed in the wind. I couldn't see her eyes behind the dark sunglasses.

She spotted me and screeched to a stop several yards away.

She stood up in the Hummer and yelled in my direction. "What in hell are you doing out in the Eureka Dunes?" she said. "A man could die out here."

"Not anymore," I said, smiling. "Can I have a lift?"

EIGHT
THE CROCK O' GOLD

"You are one stupid son of a bitch," Jane Silverheels said. "Not many people drive down that road. You need four-wheel drive to make it. Good thing for you I felt adventurous. Otherwise, the buzzards would be picking your bones right now."

I shrugged. "I'm just lucky, I guess," I said.

"Just crazy is more like it," she observed. "What did you say your name was again?"

"Shawn O'Gale," I replied. "My friends call me Shawn."

"Well, Shawn, you must be the luckiest Irishman in this whole godforsaken desert."

"I expect I am."

She looked at me and frowned. Her nose crinkled in a charming way when she did it. "Shit," she said, shaking her head.

I had to laugh.

Jane had been going on like that since she'd picked me up. I couldn't blame her. It wasn't every day that you picked up a hitchhiker in Death Valley. Nor was it every day that said hitchhiker had gotten into the valley by falling out of an airplane.

I had told Jane that much—I felt she deserved it—but I hadn't told her the rest. I didn't mention that I was looking for my friend Erin, who had been kidnapped by casino owner Rodrigo Botticelli—known to his friends and associates as Mr. B. I didn't mention being strong-armed by Botticelli's goons into a plane. I didn't mention the crash. What was the point? She didn't believe what I'd told her anyway. She thought I was just some crazy Anglo who got into the desert and over his head.

I thought she was charming. Jane was taller than me and rail thin. She had long black hair, piercing brown eyes, and angular features. She dressed nicely, in jeans and a denim jacket. She wore a silver belt and a black leather hat with a silver and turquoise headband. Tooled leather boots adorned her feet. She caught me looking at her.

"I know what you're thinking," she said. I doubted that she did, but I let her go on. "You're thinking that I look like a typical Indian. Well, bullshit."

She tightened her grip on the wheel of the Humvee and pressed down the gas pedal. Jane liked to drive fast, and she liked to drive with the Hummer's top down, even in the desert. The heat and dust didn't seem to bother her.

"Well," she continued, "sometimes you gotta play to the marks."

"Excuse me?" I said, genuinely puzzled now.

"The marks," she said. "The people I'm going to Reno to meet."

I hadn't asked why she was going to Reno when she picked me up. I figured I was lucky just to find someone passing through the Eureka Dunes, and even luckier she happened to be going my way.

"What people?" I asked, hoping she wouldn't say Rodrigo Botticelli. She didn't.

"A consortium of businessmen and casino owners," she said, talking loudly so I could hear her over the Humvee's engine and the roar of the wind. "I haven't met them yet, but they're pretty high rollers. They're interested in bringing gambling to my reservation. I'm supposed to feel them out—see how full of shit they are."

"People in Reno are only a little less full of shit than people in Vegas," I said.

She laughed. It was a nice laugh.

"You're all right, Shawn," she said. "For a crazy white man I found wandering in the desert."

"I wasn't wandering," I said. "I was waiting for a lift. And you're wrong about what I was thinking. The only thought I had about your clothes was that you looked good in them."

She turned to me and smiled. I wished I could see her eyes better behind the dark glasses, but I'd only gotten a glimpse when she first picked me up. Then, she'd tilted the glasses onto her forehead to make sure I wasn't a mirage. Much to her surprise, I wasn't.

"Thanks, Shawn," she said. "But it's a costume. People expect Indians to look a certain way. We try not to disappoint them."

"Especially when you're looking for start-up money," I said.

"Yeah," she said, "especially then." She smiled at me again. I smiled back and then pulled out my gold pocket watch to check the time.

"Don't tell me you have a schedule to keep," Jane said. Noticing the intricate designs on the watch case, she added, "Nice watch. Is it old?"

"Very old," I said.

"Family heirloom?" she asked.

"Only since I got it," I said.

"It's nice to start new traditions," she said. "I think casinos are becoming a new tradition for my people."

"A better tradition than being poor," I said.

We looked at each other and smiled. Then both of us turned our eyes to the road ahead.

Before long, we left Death Valley behind. We crossed back into Nevada from California and headed up Route 95 toward Reno. With Jane Silverheels behind the wheel, the hours and miles fairly flew by.

By sunset, we had Reno in sight. It rose out of the twilit hills like a jewel. Vegas in miniature. A little more homey, but make no mistake: they want your money just as bad.

"Where can I drop you?" Jane asked.

"The Crock O' Gold casino," I said.

"You got friends there?" she asked.

"Maybe," I said. "I'll find out once I get there."

She gave me a puzzled smile.

"You know, Shawn," she said, "I can't figure you out."

"Maybe I can explain to you over a drink sometime," I said.

Jane nodded. "I'd like that," she said. "I'm staying at the Eldorado, if you get the chance."

"Thanks," I said. "If things work out, I'll look you up."

She dropped me off outside the Crock O' Gold. I waved good-bye. Then I ducked around the side of the hotel, looking for an alternate entrance.

It was possible Mr. B had his guards on the lookout for me. It was equally possible he thought I'd died in the plane crash—someone must have reported it by now. Either way, I figured I increased my odds of surprising him by avoiding the front entry.

Fortunately, hotels always have staff entrances. It didn't take much for me to sneak inside using the beverage service as cover. I just borrowed a barrel from the delivery truck, put it on a hand cart, and wheeled it—and myself—into the hotel's kitchens.

Once there, I lost the cart and found my way to the service corridors. You have to get pretty deep into a hotel's bowels before security starts looking funny at you. Most of the time, they figure you're just a lost guest. Nobody wants to hassle a guest—it's bad for business.

So, I wandered the back hallways for a while, scoping the place out. Occasionally, a friendly staff member would try to set me back on my way. I'd take the advice only until I was out of sight. Then I'd return to my business.

Soon I had a pretty good idea where I'd find Botticelli's office. Bumping into a maid while pretending to ask directions provided me with the keys I needed. I took the private elevator to Botticelli's office suite on the seventeenth floor.

As it was late, I didn't encounter any secretaries or other interfering personnel. After all, the elevator was private, and I don't think they expected a guy in a leather Celtics starter jacket to lift the keys that made it work.

The stolen keys helped with the elevator, but not the doors on the executive suite.

I picked the first door lock and went inside. The outer office looked similar to the one I'd seen in Vegas: efficient, nondescript. I held out more hope for the inner office. I went to the door. It wasn't locked. I turned the latch and kicked the door open.

"My, my, my," said Botticelli, his voice sounding not so different in reality than it did when electronically altered. "No need to be so melodramatic, Farrell."

There was a high-backed leather chair behind an oak desk on the other side of the room. A tarot forecast had been laid out on the desk's green velvet blotter in front of the chair. The chair was turned away from me. I could see a mop of black hair and the elbows of a gray pinstripe suit, but that was it.

"Bastard!" I said. "What have you done with Erin?"

I stepped forward, leaned across the desk, and spun the chair to face me.

"I said, what have you done with—?" I never finished the question.

The man seated in Botticelli's chair stared back at me—or stared through me. He didn't react to my presence, didn't flinch when I spun his chair around. He didn't even seem to know I was there. Though he was breathing, he didn't actually seem to be alive.

I stared into his blank face and said, "What the hell. . . ?"

Musical laughter drifted to my ears, and I turned to see a secret panel slide open in the left-hand wall. Someone stepped through.

"Well, shit," I said. "I should have known."

NINE

THE END OF THE RAINBOW

"It's been a long time, Farrell Shawn O'Gale," the woman facing me said.

I tried to remain calm, though I felt anger welling up in my guts. "So," I said, "what are you calling yourself currently?"

"Maureen," said the woman. She had long silver-blonde hair and shocking purple eyes. She wore a pale violet, diaphanous gown that clung to her perfect figure and shimmered in the office's dim light. "How about you?"

"Still Shawn," I said. "My people don't change names the way they change clothes—not usually anyway."

"Well, Shawn, you can call me whatever you're comfortable with."

"Maeve, then," I said. "At least when we're in private. It seems more natural since that's the name you were using when I got to know you."

She shrugged, and her hair danced around her shoulders. "Sorry about the Farrell business," she said. "I know how it annoys you when people call you that."

"I figure that was part of your plan—to keep me off balance."

Maeve shrugged again. "It worked, didn't it? Admit that you never suspected I was behind all this."

"It's not your style," I said. "I'll grant you that."

"Would you like a drink?" she asked.

I didn't need alcohol clouding my judgment around Maeve; I had trouble handling her when I was sober. I shook my head.

"Do you mind if I do?"

I shook my head again. She pulled open one of Botticelli's desk drawers and took out a very old bottle of wine and a glass for herself.

"Who's the zombie?" I asked. "The real Rodrigo Botticelli?"

She poured her glass of wine and smiled at me. "There is no real Rodrigo Botticelli. He's always been me." She turned and walked back toward her secret panel.

I followed. As I've said, Maeve was tricky, and I didn't want to lose her. I'm sure she counted on that; she liked to lead me around.

"Oh? Who's this, then?" I asked, indicating the half-dead thing in the chair.

"Tell him who you are, dear," she said, turning toward the zombie.

"I'm Rodrigo Botticelli," the man replied in a flat, colorless voice, "owner of the Crock O' Gold chain of casinos." I noticed that Maeve mouthed the words as the zombie spoke. When she took a drink, Botticelli mimicked her movements, though he didn't have a glass in his hands.

"All right, I'm stupid, I admit it," I said. "Care to explain?"

Botticelli slumped back into his chair as Maeve walked over to me. She ran her long fingers through my red hair. "Oh, Shawn," she said, "I would never call you stupid. I like you far too much for that. Botticelli's a simulacrum—highly useful in situations like this. I can't spend all my time running casinos, you know."

"So, he's not a real person?" I asked.

"Not in any way." She smiled at me. "He's not even anatomically correct."

"I'm surprised you overlooked that little detail."

She frowned, but not seriously. "Now, Shawn, no need to be catty. Why don't you join me in my office?" She walked to the secret panel and stepped through. I followed.

The room on the other side of the panel looked normal enough, though I had the feeling it was too large for the space on the floor plan. In contrast to Botticelli's outer office, it had lavish furnishings, most of which looked to be antiques. There was a pale blue silk couch flanked by art nouveau tables, topped with Tiffany lamps. A beautiful East Indian rug graced the floor. Tapestry-like curtains covered one wall, hiding—I assumed—tall windows. A cherry-wood rolltop desk stood against the right wall. A computer terminal sat on an art deco table next to the desk. The wall opposite the desk was dominated by a floor-to-ceiling reproduction of Primavera by Botticelli—the artist, not the simulacrum.

Maeve crossed to the tapestries, pulled one back, and looked out a window. I stayed near the door, not wanting to venture too far inside her realm.

"Nice painting," I said, indicating the Botticelli. The work on it was exquisite; I'd seldom seen as good a reproduction.

Maeve turned back to me and smiled. "We had a devil of a time getting him to do it. He was quite good before he found religion."

"Are you telling me that's an original Botticelli?" I asked.

She nodded. "Of course. He didn't want to repeat himself, but you know how persuasive we can be."

Now it was my turn to nod. I knew Maeve's persuasive powers very well. Even now, years after I broke off with her, I could still feel her charms pulling at my heartstrings.

"So," I asked, fighting down the old feelings, "how long have the Fey been into casinos?"

"Oh, you know us. We dabble in everything. I guess we've owned this place since about 1972. It's so hard to keep track of time."

"Not a recent development, then?"

She smiled. "Oh, no. This isn't about you, if that's what you're thinking."

"You'll let my friend go, then?"

Maeve's brow crinkled. "Your friend?"

"Erin. The girl your goons kidnapped," I said, finally bringing the conversation to where I wanted it to go.

Maeve laughed, a light, musical sound. "Oh . . . her. She's not good enough for you, you know—a vain, self-centered creature."

That was like the pot calling the kettle black, but I let it pass. "What is it you want, Maeve?"

"I think you know what I want. You still have it?"

"Of course."

"I deduced as much from the reports. You're very conspicuous, you know, though I wasn't sure you survived the plane crash. I'm glad you did. Can I see it?"

"Not until I see Erin."

"I'm only doing this as a favor for the rightful owners," she said.

I cut her off. "I am the rightful owner. The sooner those little bastards get that through their thick Irish heads, the better."

"Now, is that any way to talk?" she asked. "They're my kin, you know—and almost cousins to you. And, despite everything, they're still very fond of you. They've authorized me to make you a very generous offer on their behalf."

"If you're willing to pay for it, why take Erin?"

She shrugged. "Incentive? Just to make sure you'd pay attention?"

"You've got my attention. But that's all you've got. You're not getting anything more—not even a glimpse of it—until I've seen Erin. She's safe, I assume?"

"Of course."

"Well, then . . . ?"

Maeve opened her hands in a mea culpa gesture. She smiled and shrugged. At times like this, I could almost believe she was human.

"All right," she said, "I'll take you to her."

TEN
FAERIE LUCK

The worst thing about Maeve is that it's almost impossible to know when she's telling the truth. Centuries of practice have made lies roll off her tongue like honey. That was one reason I disliked playing poker with her.

Another reason I disliked playing games with her was that, like so many of her people, she cheated. Not that she meant to, really. She just didn't understand that the rules applied to her. So few rules did, after all.

Still, she was as good as her word that day. Somehow, night had turned to morning while she and I spoke in her office. I didn't question it. Things like that happened when you spent time with Maeve.

She'd been smart when she stashed Erin. She'd put my lady friend in a hotel in Sparks, one of Reno's suburbs. I guess Maeve figured I might find Erin if she kept her close at hand. Moving Erin elsewhere decreased my odds.

The hotel she'd hidden Erin in wasn't flashy, but it was nice. It had enough rooms that no one would notice one lone pretty girl among the multitudes. I suspect Maeve probably had a controlling interest in the place, but I've no proof of that. Maeve liked to have her fingers in a number of pies at once.

Maeve opened the door to Erin's suite for me. It was a pretty big set of rooms—larger than mine at the Silver Sands, and better appointed. It had two outer "living rooms," each opening onto the hotel hallway. The living rooms were separated by a door, which stood slightly ajar. Beyond the room where we stood I could see a bedroom. I assumed there was a matching bedroom on the other side, probably with a shared bathroom and Jacuzzi between the two. Like I said, nice.

Erin, dressed in a long University of Nevada T-shirt, was sitting on the living room couch as we entered. When she spotted me, she jumped up, bounced across the plush carpet, and gave me a big hug.

"Shawn," she said, "I was wondering when you'd get here. What kept you?"

I hugged her back, glancing at Maeve as I did so. Maeve smiled that annoyingly superior smile of hers. I crinkled my nose and frowned at her.

"I got tied up," I said.

The room was littered with new boxes from expensive clothing stores. It looked as though Erin had been on a shopping spree. The best way to kidnap someone was not to let her know she'd been kidnapped.

"This has been great," said Erin. "Much better than Tahoe. I'm so glad you changed your mind. At first, when the limo came, I wondered, but then I thought—what the hell—you could afford it."

"Sorry I kept you waiting," I said.

She slapped me playfully on the cheek. "Brute. When Maureen said you were going to be delayed, she told me I could charge a few things. That's so nice."

I glanced from Maeve—Maureen—to Erin, and then back again. "Could you leave us alone for a few minutes?"

Maeve nodded. "Why don't you use the bedroom?"

"Great idea," Erin said. She took my hand, dragged me into the other room, and closed the door behind us. As soon as it swung shut, she put her arms around my neck and planted a long, passionate kiss on my lips. "That's for a fabulous weekend."

"But I haven't even been here."

She shrugged. "But it's still been great."

"Erin, are you okay?"

"Of course. Why wouldn't I be?"

"Did Maeve ... Maureen do or say anything ... ?"

"Like what?"

"Like tell you why you were brought here?"

She looked at me funny. "Well, I know we said that this wasn't going to be anything permanent, and I still know that. I just figured you wanted to up the ante some. All that about you being a penniless traveler was just bullshit, eh?"

I shook my head. "No. Honestly. Maureen arranged all this. I had nothing to do with it."

"Maureen's sweet. How long has she been with your firm?"

"She's not with my firm. I don't have a firm. She's . . . an old friend."

Erin frowned and crossed her arms over her chest. "How old?"

"Old enough to just be a friend."

"Okay," Erin said. She backed away from me. "Look, Shawn, you're starting to freak me out. I've had a good time, but now things are getting weird."

"You're telling me," I said.

She stopped near the window and looked back at me. "Are you saying that this wasn't your idea? That this Maureen woman set it all up? That she doesn't work for you?"

I shook my head. "No. She doesn't work for me."

Now Erin looked frightened. "Shawn, what is going on here?"

I sat down on the king-sized bed and patted a spot next to me. "Sit down, and I'll tell you."

"The truth?" she asked.

I nodded. "I owe you that much. But you probably won't believe me."

She sat down beside me. "Try me," she said skeptically.

"Well, it all began in Ireland. . . . I was just out of college, on a kind of pilgrimage, seeking my roots and all that. Up in County Cork, I fell in with an . . . odd crowd."

"How odd?" she asked, eyeing me warily.

"No drugs or anything like that. Just some . . . people Maureen introduced me to. I'd met her on the continent earlier that year.

We hung out while I traveled. I liked to party. Her friends did, too. How was I to know they were leprechauns?"

"W-wait a minute. . . . Did you say leprechauns?"

I nodded. "Yes, leprechauns."

Erin looked nervous. "So . . . " she said, "then Maureen is a leprechaun?"

"No," I said. "She's a faerie. They're kind of half-cousins."

"You mean she's gay?"

I shook my head, sounding more impatient than I intended to. "No, no, no. She's one of the Fey—like in *A Midsummer Night's Dream*."

"The movie? The one with Michelle Pfeiffer and Kevin Kline? That Shakespeare thing?"

I could see she was having real trouble wrapping her mind around this. I could hardly blame her. If it hadn't been my life, I'd have had trouble with it, too. "Yes, like that, but real."

"Shawn . . . that's just a movie."

"Yes. But it was a play before it was a movie. And before it was a play, it was real."

"Shawn . . . are you on some kind of medication? Or are you supposed to be?"

"No. Just listen. I fell in with the leprechauns. They were a lot of fun to party with. They like to gamble, too."

"Leprechauns gamble."

"Like high rollers in Vegas."

"And you hung out with them."

"Yes."

"I think I'd better leave now."

"No. Don't leave. Let me finish. Then you can go if you want."

"Okay, but could you cut to the chase?"

I frowned and tapped my foot. This was more difficult than I'd thought it would be. However, I had promised to tell her. "The upshot is, I won the watch from them."

"Your gold watch? The one with the pretty design on the case?"

"Yes." I pulled it out of my pocket and flicked it open. "This one."

"You won it from the leprechauns."

"Yes. Fair and square. They weren't too happy about it."

"Why not?"

"It was their king's favorite. It's a magic watch. It's very lucky." I slipped the watch back into my pocket.

Erin backed away from me on the bed, putting some distance between us. "Now wait a minute. Are you trying to tell me that you have a lucky watch that allows you to win at the tables in Vegas?"

"I'm pretty lucky on my own, but, yes. Among other things, it makes me nearly unbeatable in Vegas, or Reno, or wherever."

"But I beat you at roulette, that last spin."

"Did you?" I asked. "I'd say I came out ahead." I smiled winningly at her.

A look of understanding broke over her face. She shook her finger at me in a scolding manner. "I'm not saying that I buy this, Shawn. Assuming I do, though, what does your watch have to do with my being here?"

"The leprechauns want the watch back. They weren't supposed to be putting it up for stakes in the first place. So, they contracted with Maev . . . Maureen to get it for them."

"Because of the Shakespeare thing."

"Right. But she can't just take it from me. That's against the rules."

"What rules?"

"The magical faerie rules that govern these kind of things."

"Like gambling."

"Yes, like that."

"Well . . . Shawn . . . " Erin said. She wiped her palms on her legs as if she was trying to rub off something unpleasant. "I can't say it hasn't been fun, because it has. And I really appreciate all that you've done for me, even if Maureen did most of it—aside from the sex, I mean. But I think that maybe this is where I should say good-bye."

"Fine," I said. "I don't blame you."

"Good," she said. "I'll just put on my things, then, and take off. No hard feelings."

"None," I said. "I'll just clear things with Mae—Maureen."

Erin looked at me, frightened. "You think she might try to stop me?"

"Oh, no. It's me she really wanted anyway. Now that I'm here, she won't give you any trouble. She's really pretty reasonable, for a faerie."

"Right. If you say so."

I stood up and headed for the door to the room where Maeve was waiting. "I'll let you dress," I said.

She caught me from behind before I left and gave me a warm hug. "Sorry things didn't work out the way we planned," she said sincerely.

I turned and kissed her. "Me, too."

We lingered a moment. Her hands played up and down my body for a few seconds, and I remembered why I'd invited her to Tahoe for the weekend. I fought down a pang of regret. Then I went out and closed the door behind me.

Maeve smiled that superior, faerie smile at me as I came out. "So," she said, "how'd it go?"

"About how you'd expect."

"That bad."

"Yes."

"Sorry, Shawn," she said. "I didn't mean to screw up your love life." For a moment, I believed she meant it.

"That's all right, Maeve," I said. "I know you didn't mean to."

She nodded at me and then propped her hands on her perfect hips. "So, now that you've seen your friend is all right, can we get down to business?"

"I'm not giving up the watch, Maeve."

She sat down on the couch. I sat down in a chair opposite her.

"Don't say no until you've heard the king's offer," she said.

"Look, I like the old boy, and we had some great times together, but I won the watch fair and square, and that's it."

"He says he'll fill a rowboat with gold for you in exchange for the watch."

I laughed. "I'm in Reno. I can win a boatload of gold without even trying—as long as I have the watch."

"You have it on you now?" Maeve asked.

"Of course. I never let it out of my sight."

"Show it to me."

I looked at her suspiciously.

"You promised you would after you'd seen your lady friend."

"All right," I said. I fished into my pocket for it.

I looked at Maeve; she read the shock on my face.

"What is it?" she asked.

I pulled my hand out of my pocket and opened my fist. There was nothing inside. Nothing. "It's gone!"

ELEVEN
BLACK RUSSIANS

"Is this some kind of joke?" Maeve asked, her face turning deadly serious.

I was too busy looking in my other pockets to answer. I came up empty; my gold watch, the one I'd won from the leprechauns, was gone.

"Shawn O'Gale . . . !" she said angrily. "I don't know what kind of shit you're trying to pull, but it won't work. You never could beat me fairly! They knew that. That's why they hired me."

"Maeve, calm down," I said. "I'm not yanking your chain. It's gone. It's really gone."

"Well, where is it?"

"How do I know? You're the mind reader. Why don't you cast your tarot or something?"

"If I could have tracked you down with the cards, I would have done it long ago."

"I know that. Just shut up and let me think a minute."

She crossed her lovely arms and stood silently, her purple eyes flashing.

"Shit," I said.

"What?"

"I know who took it."

"Who?"

"She did."

"The girl?"

"Yes. Erin. I looked at it when we were talking in the bedroom. She gave me a hug. Now it's gone."

I ran to the bedroom door and threw it open. No Erin. She must have sneaked out through the adjoining suite right after we spoke. She hadn't even taken her expensive new clothes with her. I walked into the room and looked around futilely.

Maeve followed me in. "Why would she take it?" she asked.

"I told her what it was."

Maeve looked stunned. "You . . . ! Why in Auberon's name did you do that?"

"I felt I owed her a full explanation of why you kidnapped her."

"I didn't kidnap her. You can't blame this on me."

Fighting with her felt a bit too much like old times. "I'm not blaming you," I said, "but you did kidnap Erin, whether you call it that—whether she knew you were doing it—or not. You and I both know you kidnapped her to get to me."

Maeve clenched her fists and stalked around the room, her silver-blonde hair blowing in an unseen wind. "Mortals!" she said. Her eyes were really blazing now. She looked lovely and intensely dangerous.

I felt very fortunate she didn't have any talent for combat magic.

She spun on me. "Where would she go with it?"

"How should I know?"

"You were sleeping with her. . . ." she said.

"I slept with her once. Neither one of us planned to make it a long-term commitment."

"You've never been good at commitments," Maeve noted, sneering.

"And you have?"

That stung her. She calmed down a bit. "We've got to figure out where she's gone," she said. "We've got to get the watch back so I can win it from you fairly and not spoil the magic." She sighed. "At least the watch won't do her much good."

"Erin doesn't know that," I said. "She might be hitting the craps tables even as we speak."

"If she is, I can find her," Maeve said. "I have contacts."

"Well, try your contacts. I'll see what I can turn up as well."

"What are you going to do?" she asked.

"What I usually do," I replied, "wing it and hope I get dealt a good hand."

"That's a lot less likely without the watch."

"We'll see," I said. "I won the watch from King Beru fairly, remember?"

"So you say."

I scowled at her, turned, and walked back through the living room and out the door.

Five hours later, I was thinking perhaps I should have stuck with Maeve. She could be a pain in the ass, but she was okay so far as faeries went. At least she didn't turn people into toads when she got angry. If she had, I'd have been small and warty long ago.

I'd checked a lot of Reno on foot and more from the back seats of numerous cabs. I scoured for Erin everywhere I could think of. I even called my room at the Silver Sands back in Vegas. They wanted to know if I was coming back. I told them I would in a day or two. They said they'd hold my stuff—what little there was—behind the desk until my return.

I'm sure they thought I was cutting out. Of course, they didn't know how much money I had stashed in their safe-deposit box. I had no intention of leaving that much cash just lying around. At the moment, though, I had bigger worries.

I hung up the phone in the Eldorado—which is where I'd been when I thought of calling the Sands. I was about to cash in and head back to Maeve's when a familiar voice called to me across the arcade.

"Shawn O'Gale," the voice said, "how's it hanging?"

I turned to see Jane Silverheels walking through the rows of slot machines in my direction. She was wearing a black leotard, hip-hugger jeans, and low black boots. She looked great. I smiled at her. I'd forgotten she was staying at the Eldorado.

She smiled back and shook her long black hair off her shoulders.

"I've had better days," I said. "How's about you?"

"Boffo," she replied. "My meetings have gone really well. The tribe is happy. Our backers are happy. I even have some free time. If you still want to buy me that drink . . . ."

I shook my head. "Sorry, Jane. I'd love to, but I can't. I'm looking for something."

She raised her dark eyebrows quizzically. "Something, or someone?"

"Both, actually: my gold watch and the girl who took it."

"The girl, the gold watch, and everything," she said, smiling.

I got the movie reference. "Something like that," I said.

"Wait a minute . . . " she said, her brow furrowing. "You mean that antique watch you had when I picked you up in the desert?"

"That's the one. Do you know something about it?"

"Well . . . It could be nothing."

I took her by the shoulders gently; she didn't object. "Please, Jane. It's very important."

"I saw a watch like that today . . . though it could be another watch. I didn't get a very good look."

"It's one of a kind," I said. "Where did you see it."

"Well, one of the people I met with today is Nikolas Romanov. Do you know who he is?"

"No," I said.

"He runs the Czar's Treasure casino here in Reno, and the Czar's Treasure II in Vegas. Depending on who you ask, he's either the 'Black Russian' or the 'Mad Russian.' He claims to be descended from the Russian royal family—though that may just be part of his act. It's hard to tell out here."

"Go on," I said.

"Anyway, he was one of the people I talked to today. I didn't much like him. All the time I was in his office, he kept playing with a gold watch. It looked like yours."

I thought back. I'd gamed at Czar's Treasure II during my stay in Vegas. I'd taken them for quite a bit; they'd tried to comp me a hooker, but I turned them down and moved on. Another memory: Erin had worked for the Russian once. She said that if you did right by him, he treated you like a queen.

I leaned forward and kissed Jane on the lips. "Ms. Silverheels," I said, "you're a lifesaver—again. That's two I owe you. I'll have to take a rain check on that drink, though."

She blushed. "Shit. You Anglos talk big, but . . . "

I turned to go. "No. Honestly, I promise," I said. "I'll call you in the next couple of days."

She shrugged. "I'll be here—for a little while anyway." Then she added, "Don't expect me to wait forever, though."

"I won't," I called back.

"Shawn!" she shouted after me just before I went out of earshot. "Be careful! I hear the Russian's dangerous!"

I had to smile. I had a penchant for danger. Plus, even without my watch, I was one lucky son of a bitch.

TWELVE
THE CZAR'S TREASURE

I got quite a surprise when I opened the door to Maeve's private office in the Crock O' Gold casino.

"Ernie!" I gasped.

"Huh?" the brute replied. He had a nasty scar running from forehead to chin, but otherwise he looked fine—much better than I would have expected from a guy who fell out of an airplane without a parachute.

He recognized me and his eyes narrowed. "Why you little. . . !" he said, lunging for me.

"Garth!" Maeve's voice called from the other room. "Leave Shawn alone."

Ernie stopped in midlunge. I felt grateful. He backed up against the wall. I walked past him and into Maeve's inner office.

"I thought he was dead," I said, hooking my thumb in Ernie's direction.

Maeve shook her head. "Goblins are hard to kill—even human-looking ones."

I nodded, hoping I wouldn't have to put that to the test again anytime soon; Ernie nearly got the better of me last time we met.

"So, his real name's Garth?" I asked. Maeve nodded. "I should probably stop calling him Ernie."

She shook her head. "I'm sure it doesn't matter to him. Goblins don't care much for human names anyway."

I looked around her office, taking in the oriental rug, the tapestries, the art deco and nouveau furnishings. "So, is his buddy lurking around here, too?"

Maeve frowned. "Garth's buddy, as you call him, tried to kill Garth."

From the other room I heard Ernie growl at the mention of his friend. Even goblins didn't like getting stabbed and pushed out of an airplane, it seemed.

"So the other guy wasn't working for you?" I asked.

"He was supposed to be, yes," Maeve said. She frowned, making nasty marks on her otherwise perfect face. "It's so hard to find good human help."

"I get it," I said. "So, who was he really working for?"

"I don't know," said Maeve. "We never got a chance to question him. They found his body with the airplane."

I figured they might. The last I'd seen of Bert, his plane was crashing into the side of a mountain.

Maeve continued, "My Botticelli simulacrum had one hell of a time covering the whole thing up. So . . ." She shrugged. ". . . we may never know."

"Can't you commune with the dead or some other kind of faerie shit to find out?" I asked.

She folded her arms across her chest. "Sorry," she said, "necromancy is out of my area of expertise. We'll have to track down who bought him off some other way."

"Well," I said, flashing her a sly grin, "I might have an idea on that account."

"Oh?"

"And, I think I know where we can get my watch back."

"Go on . . . ." she said.

"Have you heard of Nikolas Romanov?" I asked.

"The Mad Russian?" said Maeve. "He's unstable. I try to avoid unstable humans."

I decided to let that one pass. "Well, I think he's got the watch."

She nodded, and her silver-blonde hair fell in a pleasing cascade around her white shoulders. "And you want me to help you get it back. What do I get out of this?" she said.

"A chance to win the watch back from me," I said. "Once I get it back from Romanov."

"I could just take it back from Romanov myself."

"It doesn't work that way, and you know it," I said. "If stealing it would do you any good, you'd have swiped it long ago. I need an extra set of eyes to help me find where Romanov's keeping it. Since you have something to gain, you're elected. I know I can trust you at least that far. Help me, and you get a fair shot at winning it back. Don't and, well, your little Irish friends can kiss their chances good-bye."

She propped her hands on perfect hips and said, "All right. I'll help. What do you need?"

"The first thing I need," I said, "is a lift to Romanov's casino."

Twenty minutes later, Maeve, Ernie, and I pulled up to the side entrance of the Czar's Treasure Hotel and Casino. I glanced at her as we got out of the limo. It felt like old times.

We decided to split up. She and Ernie would cover the casino, and I'd case the hotel. The first one to find either Romanov or Erin would call the others on the cell phones Maeve had provided.

Even without my gold watch, the O'Gale luck ran true to form.

I spotted Erin walking from the hotel boutique toward a service corridor. Her brand-new wardrobe made her look like a million bucks. I knew now why she'd left behind the clothes Maeve bought her. I decided to follow her.

I ducked back into the shadows as a hired goon met her on the other side of the first door she passed through. "The boss wants to see you," the goon said.

"What, again?" Erin asked.

"Now," replied the goon. "Hustle it, sweet cheeks." He tried to swat her fanny, but she skipped past him.

"Watch it, buster!" she called back. The goon merely chuckled.

Erin headed off down the corridor. I waited until the goon passed me by and then followed her. She got to a private elevator and fished a key out of her gold-lamé purse. The elevator opened. Erin stepped inside.

Before the door could close, I darted in after her. The door closed behind me.

"Going up?" I asked. "It's amazing how high you can get if you know the right people to step on."

"Oh . . . Shawn. God, I bet you wonder what I'm doing here."

"I've got a pretty good idea," I said. I flipped the switch to keep the elevator from moving.

"Shawn, I'm really sorry," Erin said.

"Skip it," I replied.

"I saw my chance and I took it," she said.

"Just like every other vulture in this rotten place," I countered.

"You know how hard I worked," she protested.

"Until this morning, I would have bought that line."

"Well," she said, "you owed me. You promised me a weekend in Tahoe. Instead, you had your girlfriend pick me up, and then the two of you played mind games with me."

"I told you that you wouldn't believe me."

She folded her arms over her chest. "And I don't."

"So why'd you take the watch?"

"Well, Romanov believes in that kind of shit. I knew he'd pay good money for the watch. I deserved it after what you pulled."

"This morning, you were happy just to have all the presents you'd bought on Maeve's charge card."

"That was before you started messing with my head," she said with complete conviction.

"Look, I don't give a shit if you think I've wronged you. I want that watch back."

"I don't have it."

"Romanov does?"

"Yes."

"Then why are you hanging around?"

"Well . . . He didn't give me the money all at once, just some credit at his boutique. He said he'd give me the rest after he tested the thing out."

"I thought you said you didn't believe my story."

"I don't, but he might."

"Be careful, Erin. Romanov's a dangerous guy. The watch won't work for him."

"Look, if it works for him, I'm in the money. If it doesn't . . . at least I got a new wardrobe out of this weekend."

"You could have had that with me," I said.

She scowled. "Yeah. Maybe. But you and your friends are crazy."

I flipped the switch and the elevator began to move. "We'll see who's crazy," I said, "once we get to Romanov's office."

We watched as the elevator lights climbed up to the penthouse. Just before the doors opened, I said to Erin, "You go first. And don't mention that I came up with you."

"Why shouldn't I?"

"You owe me that much."

She huffed in a superior way, but I could tell she bought it— and I'd bought a few more minutes to figure out how to handle the Mad Russian.

Erin didn't even look back as she walked off the elevator. She just stuck her nose in the air and strutted into the penthouse like she owned it. I flicked the hold switch and peeked around the elevator door.

The penthouse was impressive. The elevator opened into one large room, which seemed to occupy the entire floor. White sectional furniture dominated the room. There was a wet bar on the right. The far wall was composed of sliding glass doors. Beyond the doors, I could see a rooftop pool and patio. The patio looked out on a nice panorama of the hills surrounding Reno.

A large, burly man with a white-streaked black beard stood by the bar, holding a drink in one hand and a portable phone in the other. He was wearing a coal-black suit with diamond cufflinks and Bruno Magli shoes. He glared at Erin as she walked over to him; she pretended not to notice.

"Da, I see," Romanov said into the phone. "Nyet—No. I don't care what excuse she gave. Hold her until I can see what this is about. Dispose of her friend however you like. Just see that it's taken care of. Find the other one, too. He must be here somewhere. Da. Bye." He flipped the phone shut.

Erin smiled at him.

"You cheated me!" he bellowed so loudly that she jumped.

"I didn't!" she said plaintively. "I only told you what Shawn told me."

"I have seen this guy on security tapes from my Las Vegas casino. He is using some system."

"He told me it was the watch," Erin said. She was starting to look scared. "Honest to God, that's what he said." She glanced toward the elevator, but Romanov didn't notice.

He grabbed her by the wrist and led her to a nearby glass-topped table. He picked up a pair of dice from the table and shook them in one big hand. He pulled my watch out of his pants pocket with the other hand.

He threw the dice on the table.

"Eight," he said. "Now watch." He threw the dice again. "Seven. I crap out!" He grabbed Erin's wrist and scowled at her.

Now she really looked frightened.

"I saw this guy, this Shawn, make point a dozen times in a row at my tables, and you try to pawn off on me this? I could lose real money had I bet on this thing!" Romanov said.

I laughed and stepped from the elevator.

Romanov spun at the sound.

"How did you get up here?" he asked.

"I hitched a lift," I said. "I believe you have something that belongs to me."

"I don't know what you're talking about," he said, trying to hide the watch in his oversized hand.

"It won't work for you," I said. "You might as well give it back."

"Tell me your secret," Romanov said, almost snarling.

I shook my head. "No reason I should tell you. Give me the watch back."

The Russian's eyes narrowed. "I think not." In one swift move, he grabbed Erin around the neck, putting her in a choke hold. "Not unless you tell me what I want to know," he said. "Otherwise, your lady friend does not live to regret it."

THIRTEEN
MAD RUSSIANS & IRISHMEN

So, there I was, in the penthouse of the Czar's Treasure Hotel and Casino. Nikolas Romanov, czar wanna-be, corporate CEO, and crazy bastard, had his arm around the neck of Erin, the girl I'd shacked up with when I hit Vegas. Of course, that had been before she'd stolen my magical gold watch and given it to Romanov—and considerably before he decided to strangle her to get me to cooperate.

I had to laugh.

"What?" said Romanov, looking like he might burst a vein. "You think this funny, Mr. Shawn? You think I will not kill her if you do not give me what I want?"

"No," I said, still chuckling, "I think that I don't care."

"Shawn," Erin gasped, trying to pull Romanov's arm from around her throat, "this isn't funny."

"I'm sure to you it's not," I replied, "but pardon me if I have a hard time feeling sorry for you. You stole my watch—the only possession I'm really attached to—and ducked out after my friends and I had spent a lot of money showing you a good time this weekend. I suppose that's what I get for picking companions with my dick. In any case, you've pretty much used up your goodwill chips with me."

I turned to Romanov. "So, if you'll give me my watch, I'll be on my way and you and Erin can settle this between yourselves."

"Shawn, you bastard!" Erin managed to spit.

The Russian's face softened. "You know," he said, "I think you might mean it."

"Of course I mean it," I said. "I make it a policy to cultivate very little emotional attachment to people who betray me." I turned to Erin. "Sorry, kid."

71

Romanov let her go. Erin fell to the floor gasping. "Bastard. . ." she said. "Bastard . . ."

I could tell Romanov was gauging the distance between us; trying to determine if he could get to me before I got back into the elevator. It looked like he wanted to get physical.

I cursed silently. I'd gotten so wrapped up venting at Erin on our way up to Romanov's penthouse that I'd forgotten to call Maeve and Ernie on my cell phone. So much for the cavalry arriving to save my ass.

"My watch, please," I said, trying to sound more brave than I felt.

"I think I keep it," Romanov said. He took a menacing step forward.

"Look," I said, taking out my cell phone, "it's no good to you, and I'm quite fond of it. I'd rather not make a scene here. Just give me the watch, and I'll let the fact that you stole it slide. The police don't have to get involved."

The mention of the cops stopped him. Romanov's eyes narrowed. "I did not steal it, she did," he said, indicating Erin. She was still rubbing her throat and kneeling on the floor. She glared at him.

"Same difference," I said, flipping the phone open. "She works for you."

"Not anymore," he said. "She was never on payroll. Showgirls come and go here all the time. She is just another pretty face who did not make the cut."

"Hey!" said Erin.

I turned to her. "Erin," I said, "get your ass out of here. This is between me and Romanov now."

Erin suddenly realized that getting out of shrapnel range was a good idea. She got up and scurried to the elevator. The door closed behind her. Inwardly, I let out a sigh of relief. I really didn't want to see her hurt. Of course, with the elevator gone, I now had no means of escape, but I wasn't leaving without my watch anyway.

With Erin gone, Romanov's attitude changed. He backed off and became suddenly charming. "So," he said, crossing to the bar and refilling his drink, "you and I now can get down to business. I have watched you since you, how you say—took my casino to the cleaners." He didn't look at me as he spoke, but gazed over the lip of his glass and out the penthouse's huge windows. "You have a system, and I desire to know what it is. Tell me, and I will return to you the watch."

I knew that, on the spot, I couldn't make up anything good enough to fool him. Systems didn't work. We both knew it, even if he pretended not to. "Sorry," I said. "No system. I'm just a lucky guy. Now, about my watch. I'm willing to pay a reasonable finder's fee for its return."

He looked at me out of the corner of his eye. I cursed silently, knowing I'd overplayed my hand.

"Shit," he said. "That stupid cow, she was right, wasn't she? Trick really is the watch."

"That's bullshit. I'm just a lucky guy."

"Tell me the secret. I will make it worth your while."

"You don't have anything I want."

"You should not be so sure about that. You came here with two friends, did you not? My security cameras saw you three when you first entered the Czar's Treasure."

A sudden chill ran down my spine as I remembered a phone conversation I'd overheard while hiding in Romanov's private elevator. I'd been thinking about Erin and my watch at the time and not paying much attention to what Romanov said. Now the conversation took on a new, sinister meaning.

Romanov smiled.

"So, I *have* discovered something you care about," he said. "I sincerely hope the one you cared about was not the man. I am afraid he had an 'accident' trying to protect the lady."

"You killed Ernie?" I asked.

"'Killed' is such a bourgeois term," Romanov said.

73

"Yeah," I said. "Your boy in the plane had a pretty bad 'accident' the other day. Good thing I was luckier than him."

Romanov's thin lips drew back over his clenched teeth. That told me I'd guessed right about the man who'd tried to kill Ernie and me. Romanov had hired him away from Maeve. I took little satisfaction from the guess at the moment.

"Maeve," I asked, "is she all right?"

"Is it Maureen you speak of? Botticelli's assistant? We are not in Russia, Mr. Shawn. I do not kill my competitor's people if I can help it. My security tried to bring her to me for a talk. Her bodyguard did not agree with this; accidents happen. No need to damage pretty Maureen, though. Botticelli is a player here. I think he values her." He smiled. "Apparently, you value her, also."

I didn't bother trying to tell him that Maeve/Maureen and Botticelli were the same person. Some times, my life is just too odd to believe. I felt sorry I'd dragged Maeve into Romanov's clutches.

"Botticelli will pay her ransom," I said.

"He does not have anything I need," Romanov said, his black eyes gleaming. "You, Mr. Shawn, do."

"What do you want for her?" I asked, fully expecting the answer he gave.

"The secret of your fabulous luck," he said gleefully.

I sighed. "Erin told you the truth. It's the watch. It used to belong to the leprechauns."

"I do not believe you, Mr. Shawn," he said. "It did not work for me."

"It only works if you win it fairly," I said.

"Fairly?" he said, as if the concept were foreign to him.

"Without cheating," I explained.

He smiled an evil smile. "So, to make it work, I must win it from you?" he said. "Then it will work?"

"That's right."

"Show me," he said.

I nodded.

"First without the watch," he said. He pointed to the dice on the glass table. "Throw."

I picked up the dice and threw a six.

"Again," he said.

I threw again. The pips came up nine. The third time came up seven. Craps.

"That has never happened to you on my security tapes," he said, looking thoughtful. "Now, with the watch."

He held out my gold watch and I took it. My mind traced over the intricate Celtic knots carved on its case. I looked up to discover a gun pointing at me. Romanov must have pulled it out of his jacket pocket. "Just so you do not try anything funny," he said, smiling. "Now throw."

I did. After I made naturals three times and points four more times without crapping out once, he believed in the power of the watch. The Mad Russian smiled.

"Tell you what," I said. "I'll make you a wager. You put up a million dollars; I'll put up my watch and what I've won in the casinos so far. Winner take all. Either way, Maureen goes free."

Romanov rubbed his graying beard and thought a moment.

"To this I will agree," he said. "But only if I choose the game."

FOURTEEN
DANGEROUS GAME

Jane Silverheels looked at me and shook her head. "I still think you are one crazy bastard, Shawn O'Gale."

"It's Romanov who's crazy, not me," I said.

She folded her arms across her chest and said, "That remains to be seen."

I smiled at her, glad she'd been willing to make the trip for me. Romanov got to pick the game, but I got to set the conditions; one of them was that we have a trustworthy person hold the wagers. He'd brought the million dollars and my watch; I'd cleaned out my safe deposit box at the Silver Sands, paid my bills, and brought what was left. It wasn't a million dollars, but it was a fair chunk of change: enough to send me around the world several times over—enough, even, to finance one of my sister Shana's archeological expeditions.

The money didn't matter to me, though. What mattered was getting Maeve back in one piece. Romanov had her captive. She may have been a faerie, but I didn't think she was nearly as tough as her goblin bodyguard had been.

"You know, Shawn," Jane said, "this kind of shit happens only in movies."

"Old movies," I said. "*The Most Dangerous Game*, to be exact."

"Anyway, it's pretty crazy," she said. "Even with paintball guns."

We were standing on the upper balcony of Romanov's mansion in the White Mountains, just over the California border, about halfway between Reno and Vegas. The mountains crept up the back of Romanov's estate; the front looked out over Nevada's desert plains. It was an impressive place, though I hadn't come to admire the scenery; I'd come to win Maeve's freedom and get my watch back.

The idea was that Romanov and I would stalk each other through the forest behind his mansion. The first one to get hit with a paintball would lose. The winner would get all the dough and the watch. Either way, Maeve would go free.

This wasn't the kind of game I usually played, but I didn't have much choice—Romanov had two things I wanted.

The Russian came out of a door on the bottom level of the mansion. Maeve came out with him; she looked nervous. Romanov was dressed head to toe in camouflage. I got the feeling he'd done this before, though maybe not with paint guns. I'd worn my usual Boston Celtics starter jacket. It wouldn't blend in with the foliage, but it had seen me through some rough straits.

I called down to the Russian. "Maeve—I mean, Maureen, comes up here and stands next to Jane." I turned to Jane and whispered, "Either way this turns out, make sure you take Maeve out of here."

Jane nodded. Romanov and I had agreed to Jane as a referee because we both knew her. All the other people Romanov suggested were his patsies. I hadn't known Jane long, but at least she seemed honest—honest enough to be trusted with an important job by her tribe. I also suspected she could take care of herself if things got rough.

"You come down when I send her up," Romanov said. "Then we begin."

"After I make sure she's all right," I said.

He nodded and let go of Maeve's hand. She climbed the long flight of wooden stairs to the upper balcony. I hugged her as she reached the top.

"You okay?" I asked.

She nodded. "Fine," she said. She looked even more pale than usual.

"What about Ernie?"

"They shot him and put his body in a dumpster."

Behind us, I heard Jane draw a sharp breath. I nodded grimly.

"Shawn," Maeve said, "don't do this."

"You gonna witch up some faerie magic and get us out of this fix?" I asked.

"You know I don't do that," she said.

"Yeah, I know. You're only good with cards. Any predictions about the outcome?"

"I don't trust Romanov," Maeve said.

"I figured that out without being a seer," I said.

"Watch yourself, Shawn," she said.

"Either way, you're free," I said. "And saving your life squares us on the watch. Whatever happens here, you leave me alone. Tell your leprechaun buddies to back off, too."

She nodded. "I could point out that you got me into this by taking me to Romanov's casino," she said.

"And I could point out that you started it by 'borrowing' my friend Erin."

A frown creased her perfect face, and she said, "Fair enough. We're square." She leaned forward and planted a kiss on my cheek. "For luck," she added.

"Thanks," I said.

Jane sidled over to us. "Shawn, I know you said this might be dangerous, but . . . "

"More than you can handle?" I asked.

"I don't think so, but . . . "

"Just make sure both of you get out of here. I know Romanov agreed to send his staff home for today, but I don't trust him. If anything happens to me, don't look back."

Jane and Maeve both nodded.

"I'm waiting, Mr. Shawn," Romanov called up from below.

I picked up my paint gun and cocked it. Everything seemed to be in order. I headed down the steps to terra firma.

"Per agreed-upon rules," Jane said as I took my place beside Romanov, "Shawn will get a ten-minute head start. Good luck. May the best man win."

I nodded at her and Maeve and then dashed into the pine forest. I didn't have to look back to know that Romanov was watching my every move.

It wasn't a very fair contest. I never could have gotten him to agree to a completely fair game. He had a number of factors to his advantage. For one thing, he knew the estate, and I didn't. An hour poring over a USGS map while riding to Romanov's mansion in Jane's Humvee didn't really count as knowledge of the terrain.

Second, he'd obviously handled a gun before, and I hadn't. I despise the things; too nasty. I've shot a bow and arrow and a crossbow, and I know how to defend myself hand to hand, but a gun . . . Just not for me. I'd insisted on *new* paintball guns for the game, and I'd practiced a bit with mine, but he still had a big leg up on me there.

The only thing I had going for me besides the justice of my cause was luck. Now, I've said that I'm a lucky guy even without the watch, and I am, but I'll take skill over luck most every day of the week. If you're skillful and lucky, so much the better. In this case, I was betting my luck against his skill, and without the watch, I didn't like my odds.

So, I ran through the wooded foothills, trying to remember every trick of wilderness survival my sister Shana had ever mentioned to me. Climbing trees seemed out—good for escaping some animals, but not guns. Likewise, I couldn't count on a friendly stream to mask my trail. Not many streams where I was, and I needed to get close enough to shoot Romanov to win my watch back anyway.

As I ran, I spotted a shadow gliding through the trees downhill. I stopped, and my hand went for my gun. When the shadow moved away from me, I figured it wasn't the Russian. I wondered if there were any bears in these parts; it was an awfully big shadow. I dismissed it and returned to thinking about the task at hand.

I remembered that walking on rocks would eliminate footprints, so I picked that as a starting point. Scrabbling through the pines, I spotted a decent stone outcropping. Then I realized the problem with my plan. Either I needed to find larger sections of rock, or I needed to disguise my trail leading up to the rocks.

Having seen a few westerns in my day, I broke off a handy branch and dragged it behind me, trying to obscure my trail in the dusty soil. Mostly, it worked.

Approaching the rocks, I noticed a cavelike depression at their base. I checked. It was about four feet high, a foot or two wide, and went back into the face of the hill. The inside was totally black. There were some animal tracks at the entrance; they looked like they'd been made by a medium-sized dog. I wasn't going to go inside and check for current inhabitants. On the other hand, if Romanov thought I'd gone in, that could play nicely in my favor.

I dropped my makeshift broom, tucked my paint gun into my belt, and grabbed onto the ledge above the opening. I walked my feet into the cave as far as I could reach. Then, I lifted up my sneakers and pulled my body onto the lip of rock above the cave entrance. Once there, I scrambled across the rock face to some boulders up the slope. I picked a spot amid the stones. I could see the cave entrance easily, but a small boulder in front of me shielded me from view. I checked my gun. Then, I waited.

I didn't have to wait long.

Romanov came bounding through the forest, following my trail as easily as though I hadn't made any effort to conceal it. He spotted the cave and smiled. "Foolish," I heard him mutter.

Hidden behind my boulder, I grinned. We'd see who was the fool.

He loped up near the cave, took aim, and plunked three paintballs inside. A small, startled yelp came from the darkness; apparently the cave had a resident after all.

"Come out, Irish," Romanov said. "The game is over, I think." He smiled predatorily.

I smiled, too. I took careful aim at his chest. Then the rock in front of me gave way.

I tumbled pell-mell down the slope, causing an avalanche of scree as I came. I landed with a thump right in front of the cave. Small stones pelted me on the head.

The Russian laughed and pointed his gun at me.

At that instant, a paint-stained coyote leapt out of the cave. The coyote jumped over me, blocking Romanov's shot. My opponent's paintball splattered on the animal's coat.

I recovered my wits and fired.

My paintball caught the Russian square in the gut. Game over. Romanov's jaw dropped. I scrambled to my feet.

To this day I don't know if that was the coyote who owed his life to me. He ran off before I could thank him. If it was, though, I consider his debt paid in full.

"You cheated!" Romanov cried.

"I'm just lucky," I said. "Too bad for you." I tossed the paint gun at his feet. "Now, about my watch. . . ."

"Screw your watch," Romanov said. He reached into the back of his belt and hauled out a gun. It was the same damn pistol he'd pulled on me in his penthouse.

"The watch won't work if you win by cheating," I reminded him.

"I will take that chance," he said. "Perhaps I can get it to work some other way. Better, I think, than losing it completely."

I knew I was in deep shit.

In the few seconds I had to say my prayers, I spotted that shadow moving through the trees again. Only this time it was moving a lot faster—and it was heading for Romanov.

Romanov must have sensed it coming. He turned and fired, but the shadow didn't stop.

A ham-sized fist lashed out and smashed Romanov's jaw. The Russian tumbled backward. I recognized my savior.

Ernie!

Ernie pounded on Romanov's face until the Russian stopped moving. Then he sat on him. "I really hate this guy," Maeve's bodyguard said.

"I don't blame you," I replied.

"I'm getting tired of picking his lead out of my body, too," Ernie said. He pulled the bullet out of his freshly-wounded shoulder and flicked the slug into the woods.

I guess what Maeve said about goblins being hard to kill was true. Ernie seemed to have more lives than a cat.

"So, you wanna go back to see Maeve, or what?" Ernie asked.

I just smiled.

Half an hour later we had Romanov bundled up and ready for the cops. The Russian struggled against his ropes.

Maeve frowned at him and then glanced toward me. "You know," she said, "it might be easier if he just disappeared. Botticelli could cover it up."

"Maeve," I said, "there are ways we do things in your world, and ways we do things in my world. Kidnapping is frowned upon here, and I'm sure Romanov will be in the slam for a long time. But, if you want to rough him up some more before turning him over to the cops, be my guest."

Romanov looked from Maeve to Ernie and then back again. Sheer terror filled the Russian's eyes. Maeve and Ernie smiled.

I checked my watch. "Time to go," I said. "See you around, Maeve."

"And you, Shawn," she said, flashing me a friendly smile. "I'll explain this to my employers somehow."

I wasn't worried about it. I knew that Maeve could handle the small details.

I walked off the porch to the driveway where Jane Silverheels was sitting on the hood of her Humvee. Ernie had parked Maeve's limo next to the Hummer. How he'd found us after climbing out of the dumpster where Romanov's people had left him for dead, I don't know. Probably some faerie tracking spell or something. Or maybe he just knew where Romanov lived.

I looked at Jane. "Going my way?" I asked.

"That depends," she said.

"On what?"

"On where you're going and what you're going to do with that cool million."

"Well," I said, "I thought that I might invest some of it in this Indian casino someone told me about. I hear they're looking for backers."

"Invest? As in gamble? We don't even have any tables yet."

"That's okay. I'm sick of gambling."

She smiled. "And the rest?"

I smiled back. "Well, before all this shit happened, I promised myself a vacation in Lake Tahoe. Care to join me?"

"Shawn, that's the only sane thing you've said to me all week."

"Good," I said, hopping into the Humvee. "You drive. But take it slow. I've had enough excitement for a while."

She slid behind the wheel, started the engine, and gunned the Hummer down the hill and away from Romanov's mansion.

At least my life is never boring.

THE SECRET ORIGIN OF
LUCK O' THE IRISH

I wrote *Luck o' the Irish* on a bet. Not a bet at a casino, but a bet with myself that I could sell the idea. I'd gotten an email from an up-and-coming online gambling magazine that was looking for stories, articles, and jokes to help bring the publication's advertising to their prospective clients. They were looking for pieces up to a thousand words long, and they were paying a dollar a word—which was (and is) about twenty times the standard going rate for short stories. Though I'm not much interested in gambling, that kind of money seemed worth rolling the dice on.

That's when I came up with the "grand idea." The concept was that I would sell an ongoing, serialized story to the magazine. They'd get something their readers would look forward to every month, and I'd get an ongoing stream of income—something that all freelance writers long for. It seemed the perfect plan.

So, I sat down and came up with *Luck o' the Irish*, a cliff-hanger serial set in Las Vegas, Reno, and environs. (Areas I'd conveniently been to while visiting my in-laws, who lived in Nevada in the early 1990s.) The story involved a peripatetic hero, magic, faeries, a bit of art history, the Boston Celtics, and—because of the tie-in to the magazine—lots of luck and gambling. It would run for a year, in twelve monthly installments.

I plotted out the whole epic and wrote the first couple of chapters as samples. The plan was coming together nicely, and I felt pleased with how the pitch turned out. Shawn O'Gale is a fun smart-ass hero, and—as his Boston background and his love for the Celtics attests—he shares a lot of traits with me. Of course, he's younger, more handsome, tougher, and quicker on his feet than I am (at least most of the time), but literary avatars usually play up an author's best traits. Spending time with Shawn was a blast for me, and I hoped it would be entertaining for my prospective readers as well.

Pleased with myself and my story, I sent the proposal off to the magazine.

Now would probably be a good time to mention that I'm not much of a gambler. I like to play poker now and again, but only for very low stakes. The skill of poker intrigues me (I've been a gamer for over 30 years now), but the prospect of losing money at the whims of fate is *not* something I find attractive. I buy the occasional lottery ticket, but the only time I've been in casinos was during that trip west to visit relatives. And even then, the limit on how much I was willing to risk and lose was very, very low. I've never even been very good at video poker or blackjack. And, unlike Shawn, I'm not particularly lucky.

With all this foreshadowing, you've probably already figured out that I *didn't* land the job. While the magazine's editors liked the story, it was just way too ambitious for what they were looking for.

Sigh. Crapped out again.

Not too long after that, though, a chance came to finish the story. My writers group—the Alliterates—was overhauling its web page, and someone had come up with the clever plan of putting up free, serialized stories on the site (in homage to Dickens and our other literary predecessors). *Luck* seemed a perfect fit for that plan, and I took the opportunity to finish the story. Sure, I wasn't getting paid for it, but I *really* hate leaving things unfinished.

And when Shawn's story was done, it went up on the site one episode at a time (it ended up being longer than 12 installments), and I was very happy to have the tale finished and in the e-hands of the public.

If I remember right, it was during the hiatus between writing the first chapters and when I finally finished *Luck* that I wrote "Coils of the Python," the short story featuring Shawn's older sister, Fallon Shana O'Gale (who carries on the family tradition of going by her middle name). I had fun contrasting the siblings' personalities and takes on life.

You can catch "Coils" in *Martian Knights & Other Tales*, the collection of my short stories now available through Walkabout Publishing—www.walkaboutpublishing.com.

Eventually, I helped to start Popcorn Press, and *Luck* became one of that company's initial products: first as an e-book and then—at long last—as a printed novel. When I left Popcorn, Shawn and his tale went with me, and now all of us reside at Walkabout Publishing, where we expect to remain.

I'm occasionally asked whether I'll ever do more stories about Shawn or Shana, or perhaps even a story with the siblings together. I honestly don't know, although an idea for a sequel did begin to form in my mind recently. When that tale may find its way out of my head onto my keyboard remains uncertain.

I do think that *Luck* would make a dandy TV show or movie, though. So, if you know any producers or directors who might be interested, feel free to send them a copy.

And drop me a line and let me know how you liked the book. You can find my email along with other contact information at www.stephendsullivan.com.

May the luck o' the Irish always be with you.

—Steve Sullivan, July 2008

ABOUT THE AUTHOR

Over the past thirty years, Stephen D. Sullivan has worked as an author, illustrator, and editor for game makers, comic companies, and book publishers. The properties he's worked on include *D&D*, *Teenage Mutant Ninja Turtles*, *The Simpsons* "Treehouse of Horrors," *Star Wars*, *Dragonlance*, *Iron Man*, *Fantastic 4*, the *Tolkien* RPG, *Speed Racer*, *Solar: Man of the Atom*, *Darkwing Duck*, *Elektra*, *Rescue Rangers*, *Thunderbirds*, *The Twilight Empire*, and the *Blue Kingdoms*, among others.

Steve is the author of more than 30 published books and has contributed to numerous short story collections. For years he was the main ghost-writer for a well-known boys' mystery/adventure series. In addition to his original work, he's written numerous novelizations for movies and TV properties. Steve has won two Origins Awards—the gaming industry's highest honor—for his fantasy fiction: one for *The Lion* (the ultimate book in the *Legend of the Five Rings* series), and another for his *Mage Knight* short story, "Podo and the Magic Shield."

You can contact Steve using email or snail mail via his web site **www.stephendsullivan.com** or add comments to his blog at **http://stephendsullivan.blogspot.com.** You can also listen to his show, Uncanny Radio, at **www.uncannyworld.com.**

Steve counts himself lucky to live in Wisconsin with his wife of more than twenty years and their two wonderful children.

WALKABOUT PUBLISHING
Great stories by great authors.

Robert E. Vardeman—Marc Tassin—James M. Ward
Lorelei Shannon—Dean Leggett—Kathleen Watness—Paul Genesse
E. Readicker-Henderson—Jason Mical—Kelly Swails—Brandie Tarvin
Stephen D. Sullivan—Jean Rabe—And More!

Pirates of the Blue Kingdoms
Blue Kingdoms: Buxom Buccaneers
Blue Kingdoms: Shades & Specters
Blue Kingdoms: Zombies, Werewolves, & Unicorns
Martian Knights & Other Stories
Stories from Desert Bob's Reptile Ranch
This and That and Tales About Cats
Under the Protection of the Cow Demon

Walkabout Publishing
P.O. Box 151
Kansasville, WI 53139
www.walkaboutpublishing.com

Official Home of the Blue Kingdoms.